Trophy Girl

Melani Blazer

A SAMHAIN PUBLISHING, LTD. publication.

Samhain Publishing, Ltd.
2932 Ross Clark Circle, #384
Dothan, AL 36301
www.samhainpublishing.com

Trophy Girl
Copyright © 2006 by Melani Blazer
Print ISBN: 1-59998-275-7
Digital ISBN: 1-59998-070-3

Editing by Angela James
Cover by Scott Carpenter

First Samhain Publishing, Ltd. electronic publication: July 2006
First Samhain Publishing, Ltd. print publication: October 2006

Dedication

Special thanks to Jaci, Angie, Mandy & Shan for encouraging me to take my love of racing and cars and turn it into a book. For Vanessa for working so hard to create a cover I liked. And for S, because you raced into my life and sped away with my heart. Some days we win, some days we end up in the garage, but you'll always be a champion to me.

Chapter One

"Go high! Go high!"

Zander's heart rate kicked up another notch as he lifted his foot from the accelerator and guided his car through the thick wall of white smoke.

"Caution," his spotter radioed in again when he'd gotten past the spinning car. "You're sitting in second. All clear. All clear. Good job."

But Zander Torris, reigning NASCAR champion and favorite to win again, was not satisfied with second place. He'd led most of the race and had gotten behind with a late race pit stop. What he didn't need was this damn caution. He punched the steering wheel.

"Five to go?" he asked.

"Four, including at least one more caution lap," his crew chief, Steve, answered. "We're looking at a green, white, checkers. Scuff those tires up so you don't spin 'em. Single file restart. You've only got to pass one car, buddy. You can do it."

"I need this race."

"We all do, Z. But it's been a good day so far. We showed them how strong we are here. Lights are out on pace car. One last lap of caution. Rub those tires and get ready to bring 'er home."

His crew chief's words were hardly soothing. Passing was hard as hell on old tires, and he'd pushed these just to get back to second. At least his car was better on long runs, It was going to take everything he and this car had to pass the sixty-eight car.

Zander followed the leader into turn three, both of them weaving back and forth to get the debris off their tires. He held back just a bit as the leader came off turn four then slammed his foot down. He wouldn't be surprised if the gas pedal bent from the force of his determination. He drove hard, straining with every ounce of energy he had left in his body. Pushing. Grinding his teeth and gripping the wheel as if he could physically bully the car to go faster.

The last two laps seemed to last forever. He tried to duck under his rival on the front stretch, but since it was the best place to pass, Zander expected to be blocked. His car just didn't hook up on turns one and two, so he didn't try cutting under him. Even if he was successful, the lack of momentum he'd have coming off the corner would allow the other car to slingshot past him again.

Steve knew not to talk to him at times like this. Zander tuned out the thunder of the car and the sound of his own breathing. He focused on passing. Winning was all that mattered. All he cared about. Second place was first loser.

His rival bobbled. Barely holding back from emitting a victory cheer, Zander shot up the track and passed him on the high side, accelerated through the corner and under the waving checkered flag. He pounded his fist on the steering wheel, really the only motion he could make in the limited cockpit-shaped space. He added a few thumps to his chest, trying to calm his heartbeat. Winning was always a rush—there was nothing like it, nothing in the world. Only when he'd gotten to the first corner again did he cue the mike to add his shout to those of his teammates. "We did it! Yes!"

Zander never got tired of winning. He'd worked damn hard to get where he was in the sport—the top series, and champion to boot. Nothing had been handed to him. No breaks along the way because he'd known someone or had a relative in the sport. Granted, even with those perks, to be a champion, one had to have skill, reflex, and a lot of ambition.

He took an extra victory lap, basking in the thrill of this hard fought win. God, it felt good to be on top. He pumped his fist in the air and whooped on the radio again and again as his guys cued him in turn for their congratulations. This made him happy. This filled his life.

But as he turned into victory lane and spotted the rows of cameras and reporters lined up, a bitter taste filled his mouth. He hated this part.

"Zander, Zander," they clamored as he climbed out. He pasted on a smile and slung his arm around his crew chief, glad for the moment to compose himself for the camera. Next came the bottle of Gatorade, and sponsor props lined up on the roof of his car. He waved toward the stands, as always, awed at the number of fans who turned out for these races.

Generally, it wasn't the network TV reporters who bothered him. Their job was to capture the enthusiasm and bring the fans to victory lane to celebrate with them. Zander knew the legit networks used the race, not ridiculous stories, to lure fans.

"This race meant so much to me." He followed the standard speech his PR guy prepared for him. He credited his crew, listed off his sponsors and the race sponsor and smiled for all his pictures.

Then he repeated most of it again for the radio guys, glossing over the comment about an early wreck he'd barely avoided. He held his tongue about the rookie's stupid moves, though, only because capping off victory lane celebration with a disciplinary visit to the big yellow trailer was rarely fun. They didn't touch, no harm done, why did the media want to fire him up about a wreck that *almost* happened. He shook his head and focused on the questions he wanted to answer.

In between sponsor pictures in victory lane, the smaller press people shoved recorders and microphones in his face and the personal questions started.

"You were seen yesterday talking to Kelliann Jordan. Is your relationship serious?"

Zander pushed the microphone away and rolled his eyes. "I congratulated her on the release of her single, I think we all did. She did a great job with the anthem earlier, though. Did you quiz her about talking to all us drivers? Was I her favorite?"

One of the series trophy girls walked by at that moment and Zander made a show of twisting to admire her assets. "Oh, what were you saying?" He smiled as he turned back around? "About Kelliann? No, there's no relationship. But then again, you'll say what you want."

He turned to the next reporter, lifting an eyebrow and waiting for the next bombshell. He easily dismissed the idea he was leaving the series, but left the door open a crack when he mulled the idea of flying to the moon. He played it up. Out of the line of the fans and television cameras, he played the game, and played it well. If the gossip rags wanted to write trash about him, then he'd give them trash. He rarely told their snoops the truth, just gave them the information they wanted to write. Insulting, lie-filled articles. Whatever it took to keep them far, far from the real Zander Torris.

Steve grabbed him before he let his temper get the best of him. God, he wanted to punch these dumbass reporters for their stupid questions and even more ignorant assumptions.

"Let's get this celebration over with so you can calm down."

"I'm calm. Just adrenaline from the win, is all. Everything's great."

"I heard you're giving physicals," said a deep voice from the other side of the curtain.

Despite the hint of familiarity in the voice, Molly Freibach didn't stop putting away her supplies or even look up. It'd been a long day and she was dying to take a long soak in her hotel room's jetted tub. Besides, there was no way the two-time NASCAR series champ was standing in a gymnasium office in southern Missouri, addressing her. She wondered if her visitor knew how much like Alexander Torris he sounded, southern drawl and all.

A sarcastic remark brewed at the tip of her tongue, but she figured this was probably one of the rich benefactors who made it possible for the underprivileged or displaced children to spend a week at Kamp Kid Getaway. "Done with all my check-ups for today," she reported as she dropped her stethoscope into her leather shoulder bag.

"My loss." He pushed past the white curtain and filled the entirely too small space with his broad form.

She gasped, backing up into the table and nearly sending the containers of tongue depressors and bandages over the edge. "Aren't you—?"

"Zander Torris." He put out his hand. The sponsor logo on his shirt confirmed it. "You're Miss Molly, right?" Emphasis on Miss.

"What are you doing here?" she blurted, then slapped her hand over her mouth. Damn it, she *had* known he was one of the many drivers who donated to the foundation. But never in her wildest dreams had she expected any of them to show up at the camp. Weren't they racing in Alabama this weekend? More than a stone's throw from here, that's for sure. And what was he doing seeking her out anyway? She was a volunteer nurse practitioner here to take basic vitals, and, of course, treat any minor injury or illness. She hardly doubted Mr. Torris had injured himself.

She straightened and stepped away from the table, taking a moment to look him over. Okay, so he was a celebrity and he was standing a few feet away. Really, no sense acting a fool over it.

"I came to thank you. And see who this legendary Miss Molly is. You're all I heard about in the lunchroom today. I would definitely say half of the boys have crushes on you."

She blushed, but lifted her eyes to his face. She knew better than to listen to his words. This man was a great race car driver but had a bad reputation as a lady's man, or was it a heartbreaker? She wouldn't want anything to do with him personally. Okay, maybe an autograph—Dad would get a kick out of it. "That's sweet. And we should be thanking you. I'm simply spending my vacation here, it's the money you've donated that's made it possible for the kids to be here."

His thick eyebrows lifted, the hazel eyes beneath them seeming almost luminescent gold and green. The shadow of scruff on his cheeks should have made him look unkempt, but on him it was sexy. And then there was the uninhibited way he let his gaze rake over her, as if he were appraising her.

Oh God, no, she couldn't, shouldn't, and wouldn't think of him as sexy or wonder what he thought of her. *Bad, bad thought, Molly.* Yet her mind flew to the facts she knew. Unlike many of the drivers, he wasn't married and didn't have a steady girlfriend. Rumors flew about his love of late nights and wild parties…and wild women. For her, that was strike one, two and three. It was best she get the initial stars out of her eyes and see him for who he was—a man with the coolest job in the world and who happened to have one thing in common with her—other than breathing oxygen, of course—they donated something to the kids at this camp.

"Are you staying here on the grounds?" he asked, leaning against the doorframe and blocking her in. She made a show of adjusting the bag on her shoulder and looking past him. Didn't he hear her bathtub calling her?

"Every other night. Dr. Darrin and I switch off. Tonight's my night off." She should just excuse herself and push past him. If it were anyone else she would. Truth was, she was rather scared of stepping any closer to him. Her body was already doing really strange things—like thinking about how that scruff would feel against her cheek…and neck and…

"Great, so I'll see you tonight."

The crinkles at the corner of his eyes made her breath hitch. His lips curled in a smile over those perfect teeth, white against the tan skin of his face. Pictures and television didn't do him justice. He was tall, sinfully good-looking and had charisma that just poured off his every move.

"Tonight?" she repeated, finally absorbing what he had said. Her senses had gone haywire. Hell, she couldn't even blink. Did he notice she was staring? Why couldn't she stop staring? And what did he mean by "tonight"? He couldn't be talking to her.

"Black tie benefit dinner for the camp. You're coming, right?" He took a step closer.

"Dinner? Uh, no. That's for the money people. I told you I simply volunteer my—"

"Come with me."

Whimper. Just like that. A shiver raced up her spine. A date? Just like that? Surely he was joking. "I can't," she said.

Just a man, simply a man. His job didn't change that. Must have been his pheromones, making it all but impossible to stop looking, admiring him. Damn shame he was who he was, because there was some serious chemistry going on—well, at least on her part. Problem was, she was a huge NASCAR fan, but she wasn't even a little Zander Torris fan. He was aggressive on the track and off track, and everything she saw made him look just too big for his own ego. Without a doubt, he expected her to fawn all over him and practically swoon for the chance to go out with him. Lifting her chin, she shook her head and advised, "I've got plans."

He pushed his hand through his thick, dark hair. He always looked in need of a haircut. Her fingers curled into tight fists to ward off the desire to run them through those waves. She could tell from the way the unforgiving overhead light highlighted his hair it was incredibly soft.

So very wrong. Her mind was toast, her body insistent upon betraying her. Why couldn't she concentrate of all the negatives about Zander Torris? Why did she have to think about all the potentially good things? Bath time, then bedtime. If she were lucky, a good fantasy-style dream would give her something to hold on to. If not, she had her own methods of releasing sexual tension.

"I'd really like you to come. Your impression on these kids has been phenomenal. They're all talking about you. Heck, they look forward to seeing you. I know for a fact the boys are trying to scrape their knees and elbows so you'll kiss their booboos for them."

"They are not."

"Are too!" he insisted, chuckling. "Okay, so maybe that's the little six-year-olds, but c'mon, Molly. I know the board would want to get your impression of the camp."

Ah, so that's how it works, is it? Try to charm her into going, then when she didn't drop at his feet worshipping him, pull out the big guns and get the kids involved. "I don't think I believe you. Besides, they conduct a review at the end of the week where they'll go over everything with me." If they'd wanted her to attend the dinner, they would have asked. She'd seen several of the members of the board of directors today and no one had said a thing to her. So why *was* Zander not taking no for an answer? Likely because the moment she'd said no, she'd become a challenge.

He threw up his hands. "Whatever." She could practically hear his mind processing the fact he'd just gotten turned down. For an expensive dinner date, no less. "I'll tell them you've got nothing to say."

Good 'ole reverse psychology. She knew what he was doing, yet the guilt wasn't for him, it was for the kids. "This is the fourth time I've been to this camp. There are kids here I've seen every year. They love this place. They can let go of all the external stress in their life and just be a kid, completely equal to the boy or girl sitting next to them. This place is amazing." She stared him straight in the eye, his fame and fortune melting away as she saw the compassion burning in those green-gold depths. His media-ready smile softened, turning into a gentle sideways grin.

It convinced her to go one further. He was actually listening. In that moment she believed he truly did care. "This camp is nothing without love and hope. As long as we have that here, it will succeed. These kids find people who see them as human beings with dreams, desires, wishes, and who teach them and encourage them in ways to make them believe they can achieve anything they want. Here, none of the things society says about these kids and their ability to succeed are allowed to exist." She wasn't sure why she was telling him so much, but at least there was the gleam of respect when he nodded at her.

"Where are you staying?" His voice was rougher, deeper. His abrupt question startled her. The texture of his words sent a shiver up her spine.

"The Hyatt," she answered without thinking, then bit her lip. She wanted to take it back, but she was entangled in the spell of his intense gaze.

"I'll pick you up at six-thirty."

Before she could retort, he turned on his heel and strode out of the infirmary.

Her reaction was textbook. She stared, mouth open, eyes wide, at the doorway. Slowly, as the information digested and shock became anger, she shook her head and gathered up her bag. It didn't matter he was Zander Torris. Nobody did her that way.

She waited for him to get a decent head start before she walked out of the gym. Did she dare believe what he said? Had he come down to the infirmary, tucked back in the gymnasium office, just because of what the kids had told him at lunch? Oh, that was nuts. Yet he'd shown up here, flirted with her and then asked, no, advised her she was accompanying him tonight. She snorted. More like he hadn't had a date or the chick he was with the night before had gotten tired of his roaming eyes and ditched him. He had asked around and learned she was single and in the right age group.

It didn't make her feel any better but that rationale was certainly more believable than the champion driver simply asking her out after a ten minute—if that—conversation.

So now what? Would it really hurt to go? She still had three hours. She could get her soak in the tub and then…

Oh, hell, who was she fooling? She'd be nuts to turn down this chance. Zander-freaking-Torris. The NASCAR champion. Voted one of sport's most eligible bachelors. Who cared why he was asking her, he was. Maybe they'd get their picture taken together. Her dad would see it. Damn, wouldn't he be proud? It wasn't like she was some rabid fangirl with the grandiose idea she really meant anything. All she had to do was keep her head on straight and there'd be no reason not to go and enjoy the meal. Would she turn down this chance if it had been any other celebrity or athlete? Probably not, if only so she could say she'd done it. Something to tell the grandkids—if she ever had any.

Plus, in the scope of a few short minutes, he made her feel desirable. She deserved to feel that way. She liked that feeling, even if it had no roots or future.

She weighed the options back and forth as she turned off the light and closed the office door behind her. There, tipping the scales in her head, was the interest he'd given her little speech about the camp, about the kids. Just that hint of humanity had reached something that sort of forgave his bad boy ways just a bit.

"Bye, Miss Molly!" Several of the boys playing ball in the clearing between the cabins called out as she walked toward her rental car.

"See you tomorrow." She waved and smiled. These kids were everything to her. If she were rich, she'd spend her entire summer traveling from camp to camp, volunteering her services. Seeing their smiling faces made her chest swell—and ache, knowing this was one week out of fifty-two they didn't have to worry about food or clothes or…anything.

She paused when she heard the familiar deep voice again. At first, she thought he was talking to her, but then she realized he was only a few feet from her, just inside one of the cabins she was walking between. Even though she knew she shouldn't, she waited and listened. His tone was soft, just a hair above a whisper now.

"...the reason you're here."

"I don't want to be here. I hate it here. Hate it!"

Molly ducked when something heavy hit the inside wall near where she was standing. She should go. God, she was eavesdropping! Yet she wanted, no, needed to know how Zander was going to handle this—after all, the hot temper of this little kid seemed to mirror that of the one giving him advice. And was it so bad to learn a little more about the man she'd be sharing dinner with tonight? Smiling, she leaned against the building and strained to hear.

"Was that yours?" Zander asked.

Molly's eyebrows lifted at the calm tone she heard. Wow.

"I don't care!" screamed the boy.

"Bet you'd care if I did that to something of yours. Let's see, is this..." his voice trailed off. But when she heard the boy's frantic scream, she could only guess Zander had issued him a piece of his own medicine.

"...reason those sayings are so popular."

Molly stood on tiptoes and leaned closer to the window.

"You're nothing like me. You have no idea what it's like."

"Here?" Zander shot back. "I'd love to spend a week in a place like this."

Ah, finally. She didn't expect his temper to last, even with a kid.

"Anywhere. You don't know me or my life."

"No, son, I don't. But do you know mine? Do you know I flunked junior high grades twice and finally quit altogether because I couldn't learn to read to their standards?"

"You did?"

He did? She didn't know that. Hell, no one knew that. Otherwise it'd be in every bio ever written about him.

"I did," he answered. "I started racing young—go-karts and stuff. That's all I had, all I knew how to do, but I couldn't move past the series I was in because of my education. When I was fifteen, I was finally tested for dyslexia. By then I was so far behind in school I just quit. Biggest mistake I ever made."

Molly put her hand over her mouth to keep from gasping. Zander? Dyslexic? Seriously?

"Do you know what that is?" he asked. The boy must have nodded because Zander continued. "Later, even after I'd been racing for years—and had gotten really good at it, I wasn't getting any big deals because everyone thought I was uncontrollable. No high school education and a reputation for swinging my fists before asking questions."

"So how'd you become famous?" The boy took the words out of Molly's mouth. This story was completely different than what had ever been published about him. Had this just not been uncovered? How could this information not be common knowledge?

"Well, I could have been a bully and continued to just kick everyone's ass that made fun of me. But my dad took me aside and told me I needed to learn to respect people. And then he got me hooked up with a group of tutors who helped me overcome my disability. I'm pretty slow at it, but I can read now."

"What's that got to do with camp?"

"Can you read?"

"Of course I can."

"Would you make fun of someone your age who couldn't?"

"Probably." The boy was still cocky with his answer.

"Then you haven't learned respect yet."

"So."

Zander sounded like he could use some help. Well, she wasn't going to admit she'd been listening and jump in. She healed the body. Healing childhood emotional wounds took someone with far different training than she had.

She pushed off the side of the cabin and started toward the parking lot. Then turned back and stared at the small building where Zander and the boy remained. For a moment there, she'd seen him not so much as a championship driver, but a man facing a stubborn, confused young boy. She bit her lip.

His voice reached through the screened window and wrapped itself around her heart. "I finally took a chance and trusted someone who said they believed in me. Other than my father, no one had ever done that before. It was tough, I had to study and work and race my way up the ranks, sometimes three or four nights a week. Listen, what I want to say here is that you aren't going to get a break, you're not going to get ahead acting the way you are now. No one gets a free ride in life, kid. No one listens to temper tantrums. You've got to give a little respect to get some. And you gotta believe you're worth believing in."

Wow. Who'd have expected that of him? Sure, he was generous with his money. She couldn't begrudge him his reputation for making worthwhile donations. But more than half the drivers were active with children's charities. It just wasn't that surprising.

But in his tone, she'd sensed he cared. These kids were more than a tax deduction for him. They mattered, right down to the bully who stayed in cabin Blue Fox Four.

She smiled. It didn't really matter to her he had this sensitive side. Didn't matter if he felt it necessary to single that boy out and talk to him. Yet it filled her with a warm happiness that he felt inclined to give something back to a world that, from his statement—if it was truthful, hadn't given him all that much.

The closer Molly got to the hotel, the more frustrated she got— with herself. Regardless of what she'd heard, she should have waited for Zander up in the main hall and then simply said, "Thanks but no thanks". She wasn't one to just drop her plans for a man, regardless of who he was. She had nothing to wear, and only a vague idea of what went on at these benefit dinners. The thrill was in the asking. She really didn't want to actually *go*.

The tingling in her body had everything to do with the image of him standing there in the doorway, biceps stretching the cotton of his sponsor T-shirt, his long legs encased in dangerously tight fitting denim. And those eyes. God. Now she understood his draw.

She parked in the hotel garage and jogged up the stairs. It was useless to run from the physical awareness he had awakened in her, but she tried, Lord, she tried. And try as she might, she couldn't escape the part of her who recognized him as a grown up version of that angry little boy. Yet she couldn't quite force herself to accept he'd gotten over it, moved on and become a successful adult. Something in his voice pulled at her heart.

And it was that something that stayed on her mind while she soaked in the tub, then put on the only thing she'd brought that would be even close to suitable for this kind of event. While she did her hair, touched shadow to her eyes and gloss to her lips, she thought about the man she'd met today.

He was Zander Torris, but there was a side to him she'd never seen on TV. In fact, when she replayed the scene in her office, she realized her preconceived opinion of him had caused her to expect his demanding, macho attitude. Had he been that bad?

If she'd witnessed the scene with the boy in the cabin *before* he'd asked her, she'd have been much more receptive. Now she was curious. And looking forward to learning more about what Zander was hiding.

The media were already lining up behind his SUV when Zander got out of the vehicle in the hotel parking lot. He should talk to them, toss out promo for the camp and the brand new "Dream Come True" foundation he would be donating his time to. But he knew they didn't want to hear that. No, they were more interested in the rumors about his car chief, if his sponsor had signed on again for next year and if the recent lull in his "public" private life had anything to do with his lackluster performance on the track. He'd burned that article. And the one suggesting he was gay. Okay, that one had actually made him laugh. All these years his sexual preference had never been questioned and he went one weekend at the track without a female presence and suddenly he had jumped the fence.

Pasting on a practiced and very fake smile, he waved at the hated flashbulbs and ducked into the lobby. Could it be worse if he were a movie star? All he wanted to do was drive, dammit. That's where he worked best, all strapped in to a seven hundred plus horsepower drive machine and let loose with forty of the world's best drivers. Let someone else handle all this media shit. He was tired of defending his personal life—most of it focusing on his love life. Pretty funny considering he didn't even have one. He'd tried a relationship, with more than disastrous results. Never again. Never.

He shot his hand through his hair and thanked his lucky stars the elevator was empty.

Room four-twenty. He paused with his fist poised just beneath the number. He was early, but was taking no chances. He'd asked her on a whim. Wasn't something he'd planned until the words were out of his mouth. She was the polar opposite of what the media seemed to like to pair him with. Plenty attractive in a wholesome way, clearly intelligent and hey, she spent her vacation volunteering for kids. He dared the media to say something bad about that.

When he knocked and she answered the door completely ready, he smiled. Perfect. He knew she'd be there, and had guessed she'd be dressed professionally. Boring.

"You look...nice," he said, noting the harsh black pantsuit she wore at least outlined her very shapely figure. With a little wardrobe help, she'd look stunning on his arm. That should sell some papers.

She winced and smoothed her hands over her hips. "You're early."

"You're ready. Besides, I've got a stop to make first." He gave her his best half-grin and waited.

Molly's shoulders rose and fell, then she closed the door on him. His smile erupted and he let out a chuckle. Damn, this was going to be fun.

"I'd really prefer to drive," she informed him as she emerged from the room a moment later and ducked under his arm. She headed straight for the elevator without slowing down. "I wish I'd known how to reach you earlier and I would have told you that."

He lifted an eyebrow. Was she afraid of him? Why else did she dart away like he might harm her? "I don't think so, Miss Molly. Can you imagine how the media would have a field day with that?"

"You asked me to come to give a report on the kids, not make you look good in print," she reminded him.

He eyed her up and down, enjoying the flash of fire in her. Much better than the gold diggers who seemed to be hot on his heels at every venue he visited.

"Let's compromise here." Zander leaned in as they boarded the elevator. She wore a sinful scent, one that filled his mind with images of black lace, creamy skin and sex. Damn, she smelled delicious. She stood facing straight ahead on the other side of the small space. Moving closer, intentionally too close for her to remain comfortable, he spoke barely above a whisper. "I'll feed you if you pretend you enjoy my company. You'll get to sing praises to the board, they'll continue to think the camp is a brilliant idea, all will be great."

She crossed her arms over her chest, but he could see her chest rising and falling unevenly. So she wasn't unaffected!

"And you'll get the benefit of having a single woman on your arm."

"Thank God you're single. I'd hate to have to beat up a jealous husband."

She snorted, then frowned at him, causing her smooth forehead to wrinkle. "You're incorrigible."

"But you'll do it?"

He didn't worry that she didn't answer. Meant she was thinking about it.

"You drove, eh?" she commented when he led her up to the dark SUV.

"I *am* a driver." Did she really need reminding? And no fucking way was he going to have someone cart him around. He dealt with enough of that at the track. Hell, they didn't even let him drive his own golf cart to and from his trailer.

"Yeah, I know *that*," she replied, pursing those perfectly painted lips in a show of impatience. She even ignored his hand as he offered to help her climb up into his truck. Okay, her rebellion was starting to get old. She could at least be polite.

He got in his side. "Are you really angry with me about this whole thing?" He doubted it—she had been ready to go.

"I'm here aren't I?" she slung back, then shook her head and turned sideways as he buckled his seat belt and lowered the tilt wheel. "But then, you probably think I came because you're famous."

"Didn't you?"

"No," she retorted, leaning back in the seat and crossing her arms over her chest. She couldn't possibly realize the scowl brought color to her cheeks and the way she pushed against her chest made her enticing cleavage a little more visible. "Though you could have warned me about the camera crew you'd brought along." She waved out the window at the sporadic pops of the bright flashes.

"They're annoying as hell and there'll be plenty more at the dinner. But back to you—I'm a bit surprised you came without more of a fight. You're just jumping in a vehicle with a stranger and—"

"Oh please. Zander, you know damn well you had the advantage of your fame—yes, I know who you are and what you do, but I'm not interested in a relationship, sex, or your damn money."

"Who said anything about sex?" He didn't hide his smile. Any minute now, there'd be smoke rising from her ears.

"Just drive, dammit. Drive."

"I can do that," he said. But that conversation was far from over. Far from over. He was dying to ask why she'd come, since she'd adamantly denied all the logical reasons. He'd pissed her off. Damn, she was cute when she pouted.

She kept her eyes averted. That was just fine with him. It gave him the chance to really study her features. She had a great profile, strong, yet feminine all at once. She was too pale—the girl clearly needed to get out in the sun more, but somehow the contrast with her near black hair and dark blue eyes made her—not pretty, no, she was past pretty. She wasn't necessarily glamorous either—he'd seen too many of those mask wearing females whose appearance was shallow. Molly had a glow about her, making her almost untouchable. Well, no, that wasn't quite what he was thinking, either.

Shit. He hit the brakes and swerved to miss the car in front of him whose driver had decided to turn without a signal. "Bastard," he muttered. Glancing over at Molly, he growled at the amused lift of her eyebrows and the corner of her mouth.

"Where *are* you going in such a hurry?" she asked. "It's not 'til seven, right?"

He tightened his grip on the steering wheel and refused to look over at her. She was damn distracting and the last thing he wanted was the humiliation of a car accident. Those were bad enough on track, where they were usually acceptable. "I need to do a bit of shopping."

Zander had made a few inquiries at the front desk of the hotel, learning the location of the best women's dress store in town, then made a call. When he parked in front of the upscale boutique, Molly didn't say a word. Neither did she budge from her arms-over-chest, eyes-straight-ahead pose.

"You getting out, or do you trust me enough to do this on my own?" he teased.

"What?"

"Sweetheart, you look nice and all, but that's not nearly what I had in mind for you to be wearing tonight." Damn, she was gonna go ballistic, he just knew it. And his groin tightened in anticipation. So maybe he did have a death wish. He loved controversy, courted it constantly. But never had pissing off a cameraman been as much fun as this.

"You've got to be kidding me. Screw you, Zander. Take me back to my hotel. This is just...insulting."

"I can see you've never had a man buy you a sexy dress before." He got out of the truck and went around to her door. His patience would certainly snap if she hit the door locks. Strong was one thing, childish was another. And the nosy media couldn't be more than a half block behind them.

Thankfully, she knew the difference. "What's wrong with what I'm wearing?" she demanded, jerking her hand out of his, but getting out of the truck after he opened her door.

"It's too..." His lip twitched. Hell, he didn't know all those words the women used all the time. But he could already tell she wasn't going to be keen on hearing he couldn't see enough skin. "It's too business-like. This is a party—a black tie affair, or so they say. You need a dress, not a suit."

"My apologies, Mr. Torris. I didn't pack in preparation for having a champion driver demand my appearance at the fundraiser's dinner."

"Touché. Which is why I came early, so we could rectify that situation. Now, time is everything, shall we?"

Chapter Two

Zander's hand rested on the curve of her lower back, making it very difficult to continue fighting against his insistent control of the situation. The heat from his hand flowed through her, heating her skin, boiling her blood. He looked way too delicious in that dark suit. He'd shaved as well, a citrusy waft of his aftershave teasing her nostrils, making each of her senses beg for their own samples of this much too virile male.

Why couldn't he be a regular guy? Then she could enjoy, even anticipate building on the attraction she felt. But no, he had to be an untouchable. Someone she could lust after from here 'til doomsday and never have. Not for real anyway.

As it was, nobody was going to believe he not only asked her to be his date, but he'd taken her shopping for clothes. Sexy clothes. What the heck did that mean anyway? And how could she not respond? She wasn't dead, after all. Still, a small part of her was grounded enough to know that regardless of his final purpose, he needed for her to look good on his arm.

Ah hell. He was right. She hadn't had a man buy her clothes like this before.

The scent of vanilla greeted her as she stepped through the doorway. Her pump clad feet sunk into the plush cocoa-colored carpet. An immaculately dressed woman rushed up to them, smiling. Yeah, she recognized Zander. That had to be it. Either that or she simply read money in his tailored jacket and charcoal, brushed-silk shirt with same color tie. He could dress, there was no doubt about that. He wore success well.

After the woman had thoroughly ogled him, then made eye contact, attention was turned to Molly. She was simply going to go along with this, unless, of course, he intended to put her in something sleazy.

"Black, yes?"

Molly shrugged and looked up at Zander. He nodded and gave her one of those looks that made her feel like she'd already removed all her clothing. She shivered as his hand brushed her arm, but followed the saleswoman down to the dressing room with careful steps.

The fitting room was the size of a master bathroom, complete with mirrors on two walls, wall hangers for her own clothes and marble counter for her purse. Amazing.

"Mr. Torris has already suggested this for you." Molly followed the woman's long pink fingernail to the very elegant dress hanging on the far wall. Draped on the counter were silk stockings, panties and just below it, a pair of strappy heels. Had he thought of everything?

"He wasn't sure of your size," she said and smiled, her eyes twinkling. "I think he was pretty accurate describing. But if something doesn't fit, let me know."

"I will."

Okay, she was excited. Hard not to be when being treated like royalty. She slipped into the stockings and dress, sighing as the silk whispered against her bare flesh. Her nipples puckered as the material cupped her breasts, draping elegantly over them. She smoothed the narrow straps over her shoulders, then let her fingers trace down the sides of her curves and rest on her hips as she surveyed her appearance in the mirror. She should have trusted him.

The skirt was layered; the hem uneven. It reminded her immediately of the sketches of faeries in the children's books she kept in her office. It hugged her waist, lying smooth over her stomach. She even adored the neckline, an elegant draping of material that made it sexy, but without showing even a hint of cleavage. One couldn't find dresses like this in regular department stores, that was for sure. The straps in the back crisscrossed. Shame she'd left her hair down so she couldn't show off the elegant string of black beads that lay draped along her shoulder blades.

"Molly?" Zander called through the door. "What do you think?"

She twirled around, half in wonder, half in disbelief. "Oh my God, this dress is gorgeous."

Without preempt, Zander opened the door and joined her in the room. Suddenly, it didn't seem so big. She sucked in her breath, wondering if she'd ever get used to how powerful his presence was. His eyes roamed over her, the color darkening even as his mouth spread into a satisfied smile. He looked like the cat who had the canary trapped, and was about to have lunch.

"You're not supposed to be in here!" she cried, backing up and checking to make sure the dress covered everything it needed to. Her bra lay on the floor between them where she'd dropped it in her haste. She hated the heat in her cheeks as his eyes lazily roamed over her, then her discarded clothes, then back to her again.

She may have known who Zander Torris was for damn near a decade, but she'd only met him today. It was far too soon to be sharing this moment—one bordering on intimacy—in a fitting room, no less. Yet she couldn't deny it. Her nipples had pebbled beneath the soft material the moment his gaze had rested there. Anticipation spun in her stomach, and lower. Never had she felt turned on from a man simply looking at her—fully dressed, at that. Her heart pounded, worried he could see her arousal through her clothes.

"We don't want to be late," she said, or rather, choked out. What was wrong with her body? Around him it seemed to behave so uncharacteristically.

"I'm not sure I want you wearing that dress." Voice low, matter-of-fact, and sexy as hell. Despite the meaning of the words, her body responded as if was an invitation to strip.

Molly had to pry her eyes from the way the shoulders of his shirt strained when he crossed his arms over his chest. He'd removed his jacket. Yowza. *Concentrate, Molly, look him in the eye. You're eye candy, not dessert. He's told you as much.* "Wh-why?"

"'Cause it'd be dangerous."

Lord, she knew it was a trap, knew he said it as pure flattery but damn it, it worked. The wicked half smile on his face, the gleam in his eye. He should have been an actor instead of a driver, the man was amazing. "Well, thanks. So, Mr. Hot Shot, what will it be, the dress or my suit. Frankly, I don't care." She shifted her weight, and set about picking up her clothes, hoping to personify the confidence she lacked.

"The dress. What panties are you wearing?"

Her hands instinctively slapped onto her thighs, holding the skirt down. "None of your goddamn business." The tingling in her body pooled between her legs, making her well aware of the silk pressure of the thong's material against her most intimate parts.

Sexy, rich, who cares, he didn't need to know anything about her panties…or lack of. She repeated that to herself at least three times as he studied her.

"Well, I thought I had them pick up a garter and thong, but you're not wearing a thong with that. I'll be right back."

He stepped out, shutting the door behind him with a gentle click.

Words she usually saved for stubbed toes or drivers who cut her off tumbled from her mouth. What had been so wrong with her own black French cut bikinis? Seriously. She was slipping out of the thong—which he'd undoubtedly have to pay for just because she'd tried it on—and was just reaching for her own undies when he came in again.

"Here, I like these better."

These were low-cut, satin boy briefs with a nearly sheer lace front. He held them like he handled women's panties all day. Hell, he probably had enough experience. Good reminder, she decided as she snatched the scrap of fabric from him and nodded toward the door. "Just because you're buying doesn't mean you get to see them."

He turned around.

Her heart thundered in her chest. She clamped her thighs together, amazed her body found his presence in the room while she was naked under that skirt all the more arousing. "Out."

"Just slip them up under your skirt."

"Don't you dare move or I'll scream rape." She was really more afraid of screaming in other ways, because if he moved, it meant only one thing. Her body shuddered as she imagined him pinning her against the wall, shoving her skirt up and burying his face in her pussy. She bit her lip to keep from gasping. Her legs felt like putty. Oh, God, how was she going to survive the night?

"I'm not here to accost you, but number one, I'm buying, and number two, we're pushing late. Oh, and number three? When I see the panties it'll be because you're showing them to me—voluntarily."

What. An. Arrogant. Ass. That worked like a splash of cold water. Kind of. Her body was still hot, but her mind was no longer brainwashed by pheromones. She jerked up the panties and reattached the garters. "You're a jerk, do you know that? Fine, I'm done. They're on. Let's go."

She gathered up her clothes and slipped on the shoes while Zander paid what had to be an outrageous sum of money. The new panties alone had been seventy-two dollars. For underwear? The only thing more stunning was Zander's unspoken claim on them. She made sure to do nothing to encourage him, staying out of arm's reach and not engaging in conversation. She couldn't control her body's reaction to him, so best not to tempt fate.

They returned to his truck without exchanging a word.

Once she was buckled in, guilt took over. "I can't decide whether to appreciate the effort or feel totally violated and pushed around. But thank you for the dress."

"And the panties," he said, as if the words stung his tongue.

Both pair. The thongs were wrapped in tissue and a silver box in the bottom of her bag. "Even those."

He started the truck, glanced at his watch, then half turned to her. "Listen." Zander reached his hand across the console and covered hers. The squeeze was friendly, not seductive or patronizing. "You can say whatever you want in here, back at your hotel room or mine, but do me a huge favor. The media are going to continue to be all over us like flies on shit when we get there. I need you to smile, look like you're having fun. Make them think you actually like me—on some level, not that you think I'm an arrogant pig who's technically buying your loyalty tonight."

"So that's really what this was all about? I'm just an accessory for the sake of the media." Damn it, she knew it, but it didn't keep the sting from causing a hollowness in her chest.

"You're attractive, sexy, smart and not a fortune hunter. I'd be nuts not to want to be with you tonight. You, however, have made it very clear that given a choice, you wouldn't walk across the street to save me if I were dying. It's a little late to get a different date. And I was serious about you offering up your feedback from the volunteer side of the camp. Once this party's over, I won't bother you again."

Molly blinked at his compliments, but then shook her head. Reading too much into those would be emotional suicide. "You've got a deal."

⁂

As a driver, Zander relied upon his crew chief, his spotter and his instinct. In real life, all he had was instinct—and right now it was waving the yellow flag.

Molly went from a reserved, almost angry companion to a smiling, flirty date. She gripped his biceps while they posed for pictures just outside the convention center, her face lit up with her smile. He, on the other hand, had lost all enjoyment and patience for the evening's events. The media men, waiters, even those they'd be dining with looked Molly up and down as if she were on the menu.

She did little to discourage the attention she was getting. While he'd been able to slip his hand around her waist, hoping to remind them who she was with, it did little to stop the others from continuing to gape at her.

After they learned she wasn't simply his date, but a four-year volunteer and the camp's beloved nurse practitioner they practically salivated on her.

Maybe she'd been smart with her choice to cover that beautiful body in such a stern suit. Because his possessive nature had kicked in and he wanted to whisk her away so he could have her all to himself.

Never had he had a date command more attention than him. The photographers had even asked him to step away in order to take a picture of her by herself.

Oh, shit, why the hell should he care if the media hounded her? He just wanted them to leave him the fuck alone—and get off the obsession they seemed to have with his personal life. All he'd really intended was to use her as tonight's arm candy. The media would have a field day with the cache of photos they'd gotten. He should be thrilled. Instead he felt sick to his stomach knowing he'd just led Molly into a world of hell. For the next month she'd be inundated with people at her door, phone calls, requests for interviews. All because he'd asked her to spend a few short hours with him.

He'd never cared before. Figured the women who sat at his right hand already knew the rules of the game. Just like with Molly, there was usually a trade-off. He was generous. Money made him attractive. But he didn't care anything about that, it was all a game so he could do what he loved. His job—his passion—was to race cars and win. His obligation was to push his sponsors' products and be a role model. Role model. Christ, it wasn't even his life anymore.

"You okay?" The dinner plates had been picked up and the overhead lights had gone dim. Molly leaned toward him and laid her hand on his. The small candle on their table made her pale skin look like porcelain. He bet her shoulders were smooth, like warm silk beneath his hands. What he wouldn't give to run his fingers over every inch of exposed skin, memorizing the texture, and then start with what he couldn't currently see.

He cleared his throat. "Couldn't be better. Good food, better company." He closed the gap and spoke in a whisper. A few more inches and he could taste her. The scent of coffee on her lips teased his senses, reminding the rest of his body just how damn delicious she looked. She promised to be a cornucopia of flavors. And damn it, he couldn't stop thinking of those lace front panties he'd chosen for her.

"If you say so." She released his hand and turned toward the speaker who was taking the spotlight.

What about him? He didn't hear a word the chairman said, even though Molly's action indicated the speech he was giving was more interesting than the man who had brought her here. He was too busy watching Molly's profile in silhouette as she scanned the room, then focused again on the man up at the front of the room. As if he wasn't even there.

He was dying to reach under the table and rearrange his stiff cock and aching balls and she was flat out ignoring him. Damn, he should have listened to instinct and...and what? Stayed home? That would have fed the damn media hounds. No, he fed them when and what he wanted them to print. Heaven forbid should he do, or not do, something on Wednesday that affected his performance on Sunday. No matter what, how he qualified, practiced and raced would be directly related to the mystery woman he was out with during the week. Unless he put an end to it.

Rolling his eyes, he leaned back in his chair and downed his drink. Damn shame he was driving. About three more of those rum and colas would take the edge off his foul mood quite nicely.

"Ready?" she said, the moment the lights came back on.

More than. "If you are," he responded, trying not to seem too eager. The entire night had turned into a multi-car pileup. He'd lost sight of the entire reason he was here. Molly had nothing to do with it, but he'd wasted the better part of an hour feeding his temper.

"I'm exhausted. I don't do this elbow-rubbing thing well. But thanks again for inviting me. It was very informative."

Her sincerity wasn't an act. Maybe that's what it was about her. Molly was who she was, nothing about her fake. She didn't pretend in order to catch his attention—or to keep it. While it felt wonderful to finally be with someone who had that genuineness to her, it was also frustrating as hell.

Instinct told him he had to unload her as quickly as possible. Tomorrow he'd be in another city, at another track and there'd be plenty of those shallow, predictable women. He could pick one to accompany him to any required dinners and leave her behind without so much as a second thought.

Yet as they made their way around the room, saying their farewells, he kept his hand on Molly at all times. Heat radiated through her as he lightly touched the small of her back to guide her. As she walked, her hips swayed, a subtle yet damn sexy movement that made him crazy. He slid his fingers to her waist, where he could feel every breath she took. His mind took off on a tangent where it imagined her breasts rising and falling with her increased breath, where she panted his name as he brought her to the peak of ecstasy with his tongue.

"Zander?" she said, turning against him. His already stiff cock lurched as her body came in full contact with his side. She smelled good, felt good. Damn, he was in some serious trouble here, and no quick pit stop was going to make it go away. No, this was one of those take it to the garage and work on it for awhile type of problems—the kind he needed to avoid both on and off the track.

"Ready when you are, sweetheart."

She stepped away, breaking all contact and smiled at him. "I think Mr. Richardson wanted to thank you."

"Excuse me, sir," he said, cursing himself but reaching out to accept the senior chairman's handshake.

"No apology needed. It's easy to see why you're distracted with such a beautiful—and intelligent—woman on your arm. I think you've found yourself a winner with this one, champ."

"I think you may be right," he agreed, hating the lie, but unwilling to admit she was only here for her face value. "I trust my accountant has indicated I've stepped up my donation this year."

"The very reason I wanted to speak to you before you left. The board and I met last week upon hearing the news. We'd like to use the extra money to do something similar to the Make a Wish Foundation but with the children we reach with our own foundation. The legalities are all in the works, of course, but we were wondering if you would allow us to dedicate part of your funds, and use your name of course, to help promote this outreach program."

Molly gripped his forearm, her excitement channeling through his own bloodstream. Didn't the woman have any idea how it felt to have his arm pressed against her breast? How could a man think? "It'll have to go through my lawyers, of course, Mr. Richardson, but I've already been approached on it and indicated there'd be no problem whatsoever doing what it takes to help these children."

"Splendid." The chairman pumped Zander's hand one more time. "Now I'll let you get on with your evening with your wonderful lady friend."

"How exciting. These kids are going to go from underprivileged to the luckiest kids in the world," she gushed as they walked through the dimly lit entrance hall. Once they opened the glass doors, however, the flashbulbs started popping like firecrackers on Independence Day.

He put his head down and pushed forward, sliding his arm around her shoulders and pulling her close, shielding her as best he could. "They already are the luckiest kids—they've got you seeing to their health."

"The minor check-ups I do aren't much. I've never done more than administer a couple of stitches, give tetanus shots or treat a bellyache in all my years of volunteer work."

He didn't answer. He heard her, but was more impressed with the way she seemed to completely ignore the people standing in their way or asking them questions. When he let her in his truck and closed the door, he turned to the photographers who'd come right up to the window, issued his best evil look, flipped them a gesture he made sure Molly couldn't see, and told them to get the hell away from her.

Just when there's a light at the end of the tunnel, he found out it was a goddamn flashbulb. At least she wasn't freaked out.

"Sorry about that," he said when they were on the main road and had left chaos behind them.

"It's a mob scene, isn't it? I never realized it was that bad. Of course, I don't read the tabloids and only see some of the pre-race/post-race shows. I'm a green to checkered flag kind of fan."

"If I had it my way, that's the only time anyone would see me." He felt something click with her. "Except for victory lane celebration, that is." He glanced over, only to find her studying him with a thoughtful smile. In the light shining in from the streetlamps and oncoming headlights, he saw something in her face he hadn't allowed himself to look for in years. Since Lana.

He saw tomorrow.

No. Zander wrapped both hands around the steering wheel and stared straight ahead. Streetlights and illuminated billboard signs. Tomorrow. Yes, he'd see those tomorrow. Runway lights at the airport, fast food restaurants, another hotel. Then the track, another circular plot of land to call home for the weekend. That's what tomorrow was, not a comfortable ride home from a night on the town with a beautiful woman.

He couldn't have that. It wasn't in his present, and likely not in his future.

"You started racing when you were young, didn't you?"

"Yeah. About six. Go-karts." God, he didn't want to get into this. He avoided talking about what life was like back then and Molly would be just the type to ask personal questions. He didn't want to relive the lost feeling that had all but swallowed his childhood. The homelessness, the lack of friends, nights his parents fought, and later, his father's drunken plea for him to win just one more race so they could pay the rent on the little hotel room they called home. He blinked back the pain the memories brought forth. His bio, except the number in the win column, was fictional—up until he turned twenty-three and stormed the ARCA series, defeating the champion his first season out.

It was still about ten more miles to town. Thankfully, her hotel was just off the highway. Despite the fact he'd enjoyed her company—and hated the fact so much of her time had been monopolized by everyone else tonight had been a mistake.

"Did you travel a lot back then?" she pushed.

Something inside him snapped. "Go to my website. They tell me my whole life fucking history is printed there." The sterile version, but at this point he didn't care. Maybe it was seeing the kids today, knowing how they felt, seeing the hollowness in their eyes, and worse, the blackness of hate that had built up in others. It was a reminder, something he didn't want to remember. Certainly not tonight.

He didn't look over, didn't want to see the hurt he'd inflicted reflecting in her eyes. Guilt washed over him, pushing his own pain aside as he realized what he'd done. Christ, why had he lashed out like that? Because she'd made him feel? He didn't want to feel, but she didn't know how painful her questions had been.

Yet, when he glanced over, he realized her expression was anything but soft. In fact, it was anger, not pain that laced through her next words. "Listen, Mr. NASCAR bigshot, I was asking because I hung out at some local tracks and was curious if we had crossed paths. It was my understanding you lived only a few hours from where I grew up. You know, just making conversation here. Clearly you're too good to speak to me, considering you've gotten what you wanted out of this."

He gritted his teeth and glanced in her direction. She had her hands clasped tightly on her lap, ivory against the black of her skirt. Her face was turned away. She stared into the dark abyss beyond the window.

He backpedaled, remorse a terrible pill to swallow. "You have no idea what it's like to have to answer those questions over and over and—"

"Cut the bullshit, Zander. Just take me home."

Damn, what she did to him. The word "home" hit him like a car with a stuck throttle, wasting his frustration and anger and filling him with thoughts of a real home. Of course, parts of him thought about that real home having a real bed, and having Molly in it. Naked.

What the hell would she say to that bit of word association?

Who said the anger management classes they were all now required to take hadn't done him any good?

He didn't say anything, just stared at the damn haunting white dashes on the road, maneuvering gingerly through mild traffic and pulling up in front of her hotel lobby. The flash of anger and hurt dissipated, slowly, but with it came the dawning that to him, Molly wasn't another mannequin he used as a media prop. He cared that he'd hurt her. Which was all the more reason to let her go before he did something stupid.

"Now," he said, turning to her and choosing his words carefully. "First, thank you for coming with me. Despite the fact we're like a cat and mouse together, I can say it was overall enjoyable. And because my mother would kick my ass from here to Chattanooga if I didn't at least ask, do you want me to walk you to your room?"

She laughed.

Lord, he'd never understand women and their ability to switch moods so fast. "Is that a no?" he asked.

"Don't worry, I won't tell your mother about your manners. Though I'd be surprised if she doesn't already know better. I bet she owns a TV." Molly pushed open the door and without a backward glance, walked through the lobby doors.

Chapter Three

Molly stood in front of the elevator doors and closed her eyes. Last thing she wanted to do was deal with the mental questions. Like *what the hell happened there?*

Truth was, as much as she hated to admit it, Zander Torris was a prick. An egotistical, self-centered legend in his own mind. And when she didn't agree with his greatness, he got shitty about it. And while she was pissed as hell she didn't get his autograph as a gift to her dad—

Shit.

Her clothes were in his SUV.

She leaned back against the wall of the elevator. He'd been so eager to get rid of her he'd *asked* if she wanted him to walk her in. What a jerk. He was probably halfway to the airport by now, eager to get on his private jet and head back to the world of adoring fans who didn't question his humanity. *Well, good riddance, Zander Torris. Hope you hit the wall on Sunday and it makes you think of me.*

No, scratch that. She didn't even want him thinking of her.

She was tired, cranky, sexually frustrated and just lost the best damn black suit she'd ever owned in her life. And her favorite black bra.

The elevator chimed. Blowing out an exasperated breath, she exited and headed to her room, more than eager to get her clothes off and drop into bed.

Wrapped in her favorite silk kimono-like robe, she held up the dress Zander had bought. Where was she going to wear it again? She didn't frequent black tie affairs, and even so, it's not like she could wear it every time. Hell, the tabloids acted as if it was a sin to wear anything twice.

As if anything she ever did again would compare to a media attended dinner on the arm of—

Molly pressed her hands to her temples. "Stooooop!" she cried. All she wanted was to hit the eject button on this constant rewind of the night's events. Would she think about this for days? Likely, especially when fueled by everyone gushing about seeing her on the news. If she were lucky, something way more newsworthy than the series champ attending a benefit for a camp would break on the NASCAR horizon and any photographs containing her would be put at the bottom of page three and reduced to naught more than a thumbnail.

Of course, her father got the weekly NASCAR publications and devoured them with more interest than the daily newspaper. She'd hear all about it regardless.

And then she'd have to go through this entire mental debate...again.

She hung up the dress and returned to the bathroom to wash her face and brush her teeth with the hopes of retiring to a dreamless night of sleep.

The knock on the door damn near made her swallow her toothpaste. Crap! She continued scrubbing, thinking. She hadn't ordered room service. Maybe she'd had a message at the lobby? Still, why were they coming up here? How'd they know she'd returned and didn't they have some sort of message center hooked up to her phone?

The knocking continued. Harder.

"Coming," she muttered around the handle of her toothbrush. Geesh, impatient. And probably some moron with the wrong room.

For that reason, she left the safety chain in place. She'd discovered someone had broken her peephole—or colored over it—so it wouldn't help her.

"Yes?" she asked as she opened the door a scant two inches. Then she saw him. Not room service, not someone from the lobby desk. Zander Torris. Standing in her hallway.

She slammed the door shut, then leaned on it for good measure.

Shit! Her damn betraying body hummed with anticipation. He'd come to her room!

No. She wouldn't let him in. She straightened her spine and darted to the bathroom to spit the toothpaste out. Why should she be scared of him? She'd already decided he was one step above pond scum. All she needed to do was get her clothes—because that had to be the reason he was here—and dismiss him.

She was surprised he hadn't resumed pounding loud enough to wake the people three floors down. Perhaps he'd cooled off a bit. Praying for that, she opened the door just far enough for him to pass the clothing bag through.

"I'm sorry to bring you up here, Zander. You could have had one of your people send the clothes to the camp."

"Clothes?"

The door cut into her palm as she tightened her grip on it. "Yes, I left my bag of clothes in the backseat of your truck."

Her stomach twisted, her heart, damn heart, thudded against her ribcage. And her traitorous mind wouldn't stop thinking. He'd come back for a reason other than returning her clothes. Why?

He shook his head, then smiled. "I didn't even notice them back there."

She wouldn't let him in. No way. "Then just leave them at the front desk or send them to the camp. I'm tired and I'm going to bed. Thanks again for an…interesting night."

"Wait," he growled, slamming his palm against the door. The clunk of his heavy, gold championship ring echoed in her head, another reminder of who he was. Not a normal date. Oh, why couldn't she see past his notoriety anyway?

"What?" She hoped she sounded as impatient as she felt. Rude or not, she just needed this to be over.

"I don't give up on the racetrack when I get a lap down and I sure as hell ain't giving up tonight."

"Tonight?" she repeated incredulously. She'd have taken a step back and laughed hysterically if she didn't need to keep a death grip on the door. Though they both knew he could overpower her if he really wanted in. "Maybe you're not used to someone who's less than impressed with your star status. Actually, I'm more impressed with that—and your driving ability—than I am with you as a person. So why don't you leave me an autographed fan card in the bag with my clothes when you return them? Good night, Zander."

"Molly."

Why couldn't she be strong enough to say "fuck off" and slam the door and then go to bed without worrying about all the consequences and her mind playing the very annoying what-if game? "I thought I made everything clear."

"Well, *I* didn't."

"No."

"Please?"

Please? No, it didn't sound even remotely pleading. Almost like a child reminded by his mother to use his manners. Reminded because he never had to actually use them. He was probably unaccustomed to hearing the word "no".

Then she realized why it got to her, why she hesitated, breath held as she stared up at him through the three-inch opening.

The way he said please reminded her of the way he talked to that little boy in the cabin. As if all pretenses had been dropped and he was just a man asking for a second chance—not because of his status or his money, but because he had something to say. He could have pushed the door, Lord knows he was strong enough. But he didn't. He asked.

Blowing out her breath, she relented. It'd really been a lost cause from the beginning, but she hadn't been ready to accept defeat. Now she was surrendering only for the sake of her own curiosity. "Five minutes. That's all you got."

Zander handed her a single white rose. What was that, a peace offering? Yet somehow it broke down even more of her newly created brick wall. Damn the man anyway.

"Zander," she warned. She wasn't sure why she even tried. He didn't listen to her, just pushed right past her, closed the door behind him and turned the lock.

"Tonight went all wrong. All wrong."

"Tonight was nothing more than a publicity stunt, remember?" Molly put the rose down. It was hard to remember to be bitchy with such a token in her hand.

"No. Yes. Damn it!" He paced the floor, effectively taking over her space with his size, his scent, his being. "That was the plan, yes, but—"

"Oh, don't feed me a line of bullshit about the dress, or me or something else to try to seduce me. I don't know if you noticed, but there are plenty of women who will fall at your feet."

His face contorted, turning all hard lines and shadows. His eyes darkened, like a sky with storm clouds gathering. She stepped back as she digested the change in him. But then she realized it was just his competitive spirit. She'd seen that look before—right before he donned his helmet, and his crew put up the protective window net, sealing him in his car for four or five hundred miles. It was his game face.

Well, she wasn't some fellow driver and this was certainly no race-track. He may be competitive, but she wasn't out to be conquered. Straightening her shoulders, she drew up all of her five and a half foot stature and waited for the confrontation in which he told her all the sappy things he thought she wanted to hear. She nearly rolled her eyes.

That didn't come. Zander grabbed both her upper arms, pinned her against the door and lowered his mouth to hers.

He caught her with her lips parted, ready to tell him to back off. But she never had a chance. He silenced any retort with the powerful pressure of his lips on hers. He shifted, nudging her lips further apart and stroking her tongue. His kiss was white hot and intoxicating. She leaned back, unable to fight. Standing suddenly seemed like too much to handle on her own.

When he relaxed to take a breath, however, Molly sidestepped his loose hold and put as much distance between them as possible.

"What was that for?" It was hard to breathe. Impossible to think. Amazing she'd escaped with her life. She licked her lips and tasted him there. That kiss shouldn't have happened. What had she been thinking, letting him in here? She stifled a whimper and wrapped her arms over her chest.

"I don't want them."

Huh? "Who?" She shook her head and stared at him from halfway across the room.

"Anyone." He shrugged his shoulders, then made a circle with his hands. "All of them. The other women." Zander took up pacing again, which brought him much too close to her to be holding this conversation.

What the hell was he saying? Her adrenaline was pumping, she was way too aware there was only one, silky, thin piece of clothing between her naked body and Zander. Everything she said, thought, touched, made her think of him. How had he infected her this way? "Is this some new revelation or another attempt to lure me in the sack?" Mincing words just didn't seem effective with him.

But putting it that way—how the hell had she tried to sound accusing and managed to make it sound as if she were issuing a challenge? She groaned, but noticed he was eyeing the king-sized bed.

"Don't even think about it," she hissed.

As he turned to her, a mere four feet away, she sucked that last breath back in. His eyes were gleaming gold beneath half-closed lids. His lips were slightly parted. She couldn't help but drink in his features, wondering how a man could look so damn sensual yet be so infuriating at the same time. She longed to touch his hair, feel the soft waves wrap around her fingers. It brushed the tips of his ears and curled at the nape of his neck. God, that was sexy. As was the stubble—always a weakness, right now it seemed so much more pronounced. The shadow accented a strong jaw and ended right beneath sinfully powerful cheekbones. How dare he look deliciously aristocratic and yet devilishly naughty at all once?

He drove her mad. That, simply, was the answer.

"You need to leave," she said, without attempting to hide the tremble in her voice. "You shouldn't be here."

"Molly." The way he said her name was a caress. The throaty texture of his whisper a pair of velvet hands sliding over her body, reaching into places they had no business going.

"Go," she murmured. Her feet were glued to the carpet, her eyes locked on his as he stepped closer. "Please no."

A foot from her. Close enough she could smell his cologne and the pure masculinity he shouldn't hide with any over-the-counter scent. If he spoke again, she'd feel his breath against her hair. Either of them could reach out.

Instead he stopped and averted his gaze. She watched his chest rise and fall beneath the tailored shirt even as he studied the ceiling. There was something about him, something about that look. Then she realized. She'd watched countless interviews with him, dozens of shots of pre-race preparation where he wasn't aware of the camera, even noticed him in the background, goofing with teammates, but she'd never see him look…alone. Unsure. There was a flash of vulnerability. It was confirmed when he drew his eyes down to her. Then it hit her like a sucker punch to the gut. He was at war with himself. Over her.

She cleared her throat, jerked her eyes away and repeated what her mind had just told her. When she looked back, disbelieving, the look was gone.

"You're right. It's late and I'm sorry." He let out a pent up breath and looked around the room. "I need to get out of here. I'll call you."

He stepped forward. "I'm sorry," he whispered, touched her lips with his—a simple yet reverent gesture that seemed to speak so much—then walked out.

What had she done? Why? Had she kicked him out because he was Zander Torris, or because he made her forget everything but his kiss?

Zander got in his vehicle and sat. His favorite place in the world was positioned with a steering wheel in his hands and three pedals at his feet. Of course, his SUV only had two, but even if he'd had twenty, going through the motions tonight just wasn't going to break up the spinning mess in his head.

Something about her had gotten to him. Groaning, he glanced over to the passenger seat, then back behind it. Just as she'd said. Her bag of clothes. There was no way in hell he was going to tempt fate again and go back up to her room. Of course, he wasn't ready to hand them over to the night clerk at the desk either. Tomorrow he'd figure out what to do.

He pulled out of the lot and drove the few miles to his hotel, thankful the paparazzi had finally given up. It was remarkable how quiet it was without them hounding him. He could slow his pace, see things around him. He could actually feel like a real person.

Oh, he felt all right.

If he were smart, he'd head down to the workout room and replace the confusion, hope, attraction and all that other useless shit Molly had caused to surface. He'd replace it with good old-fashioned muscle ache.

The choice made, he jogged up the steps to his second floor suite and discarded dress clothes for T-shirt and sweats.

He ran on the treadmill for three miles. The whole time he envisioned Molly at the end of the road, wearing that dress like a second skin. The harder he ran, the worse it got. At first he just imagined her there, then he saw her taunting him, teasing him with seductive poses and sensuous moves. As if she were dancing to a tune he couldn't hear. All he heard was the thunder of blood running through his veins and the steady thud of his feet on the rubber belt.

After guzzling water, he focused on free weights. By the time he was done, his body could barely make it back up the stairs. His muscles ached with the effort of pulling his shirt over his head. He stood beneath the shower and prayed the water would finally wash away any thoughts of Molly.

Instead, his cock tightened as he imagined how much he'd enjoy her sliding into the shower stall with him. They could steam up the glass cubicle even with the cold water on full blast. His mouth watered at the idea of licking droplets of water from her firm skin, and then watching her return the favor.

He encircled his erection with his hand, sliding slowly down the base of the shaft, squeezing, before pulling upward until his grip tightened around the tip. Would she choose to stand with her hands on the wall, legs spread and her perfect ass jutting toward him, eager for his invasion? Or maybe she'd take it upon herself to hike one leg over his hip and lower herself on his cock.

Groaning, he pumped his fist, alternating between tight thrusts and loose caresses, all the while imagining her gentle hands touching, exploring, teasing him to the edge of reason.

"Molly," he muttered. Just hearing her name sent chills through his body. He sped up, wishing it were the tight walls of her pussy gripping his cock instead of his own hand. But it was easier this way.

His imagination lacked nothing. As he brought himself to swift climax, he closed his eyes and imagined her on her knees, swiping at the tip of his cock, sucking at the slit and lapping up the fluid she found there. His body jerked, an intense power jolted through his body.

But instead of feeling even remotely satisfied, he was pissed at himself for letting her steal his self-control and force him to take matters in his own hands...literally.

Chapter Four

"I know what time we're scheduled to leave. We'll make it. Relax." He clicked his cell phone off and smiled. He was on his way back from the camp, where he'd charmed some vital information about Molly from the operations manager. It was one of those rare times he abused his celebrity status to get something he shouldn't have access to. In the least, he'd use her address to get her clothes back to her. Maybe he'd call her…

Maybe not. He gunned the engine to get through a yellow light and turned into the rental car lot. Within minutes, he was shuttled to his jet and preparing for lift off.

It was easier to focus on the schedule of the next few days once he was back in familiar surroundings. When they were safely in the air, he pulled the file his crew chief had sent with him and reviewed the notes—mostly graphs regarding the track and their last performance there. It was an exercise he enjoyed, reviewing things like tire wear and the impact of recent use on the track. Since no rain was forecast the entire weekend, it'd be easier to predict handling than if the track were clean. Routine. Hectic, but the way he'd lived his life ten months out of the year for the last five years. Or more, really.

He had all but put last night behind him when his cell phone vibrated against his hip.

"Yo!" he said after consulting the caller ID. It was his publicist, probably letting him know this evening's agenda.

Not quite.

"Who the hell were you with last night?"

"Huh?"

"I've had non-stop calls from all the trade papers and magazines trying to get the low down on this so-called serious relationship."

Zander shifted the phone to his other ear and moved the paperwork from his lap to the empty seat beside him. "Serious? Christ, Pete, I just met her yesterday."

"Who is she?"

"Volunteer nurse at the camp—"

Pete cut him off. "How'd you get tangled up with her?"

Zander bristled. Pete Hargworth was his friend, one of the guys who'd been with him since he started racing this league. Pete rarely questioned his choice of companions, even when he pushed the very limits of decency. "I don't like your tone," he spat, not bothering to edit his thoughts.

"Tone? Zander, maybe you're not realizing what you're doing here. No one takes your dates seriously. Everyone knows the media plays it up. But this girl? She's the real thing. You can't go fucking up her life because you thought she'd be a challenge."

If he could reach through the phone, he'd throttle the man on the other end. "Challenge?" he barked. "I don't ever want to hear you talk about her like that again." He closed his phone. Then opened it back up, and turned the damn thing off. This, he didn't need.

Great. He wondered if the media had found Molly yet. It was going to be worse than he anticipated. At least he had the better part of an hour to think about what to say to the influx of recorders and microphones that would be thrust in his face as he left the airport, and then again when he arrived at the track.

～～ ～～ ～～

"Who is the woman—"

"Where did you meet her—"

"Is it serious?"

Zander turned, hearing bits and pieces of all the questions, but responding finally at that last question. "Serious?" he repeated, spitting the word. "Your definition or mine? I escorted a volunteer nurse—"

"I heard she was a nurse practitioner," someone cut in.

Zander growled. "Yes, she is. I met her earlier in the day, learned what an impact she had on the kids at the camp and asked her to accompany me to learn about the future directions of the camp."

"So you're not seeing her?"

"Does it look like she's here? It's Thursday. Sorry, buddy, she's back to her life and I'm back to mine. Now, care to discuss what you did for dinner last night?"

"Excuse me?"

Zander turned directly to the camera and smirked. "Never has a charity dinner been so dissected. I'm sorry, Molly. These people, these reporters are a joke."

He turned and entered the garage, the reporters kept at bay with a chain link fence. Like the animals they were.

"It's getting worse, isn't it?" Chad, the rear tire changer for Zander's pit team looked up from inspecting his air impact wrench and hose.

"You couldn't know."

"Steve said they're like piranhas today."

Zander looked over Chad's shoulder and nodded at Steve, his crew chief, who was waving him over. "Someone throw them some food then, get 'em off my ass."

"You did, man, you did. I really feel sorry for the chick you were with last night."

Zander balled up his fists, trying to ward off the blistering red heat from blinding him with temper. He needed to get in touch with her, to warn her. Hell, he could offer her protection of some sort, get her away so they couldn't get to her. At least until this blew over.

"Tell me something. Or get me in my car and on the track before I blow a gasket and shove one of their cameras where the sun don't shine." Zander walked past his crew chief and longtime friend and leaned against the toolbox. "I just want to drive. Just drive."

"It's all part of the game, Z. We don't have to go over that again. But what the hell did you do to get them so fired up?"

"Hellifino."

"You invite her to the track?"

Zander stared at him incredulously. "Are you out of your fucking mind? They'd rip her to shreds here. Besides, last night was a one-time deal. I was lucky to make it through alive and in one piece."

"That much of a wildcat, huh? No wonder you look like you need a nap."

"Christ, Steve, it wasn't like that. I'm thinking she called me a pompous ass and a jerk within the first fifteen minutes of getting in the truck. We called a truce while in public, sure, but—"

"Damn. That's bad."

Zander narrowed his eyes and put down the three-quarter-inch wrench he was turning end over end. His crew chief wasn't agreeing with him, he was mocking him. "What's that supposed to mean?"

"Never seen you defensive over a piece of ass."

Zander opened his mouth, ready to launch into Steve with both barrels loaded. Then he realized that's exactly what his crew chief intended for him to do. He closed it again and picked up the wrench, running his fingernails over the engraved manufacturer's logo. "It was a mistake. I invited her because I figured it'd be good to show up with female companionship. The kids at the camp love her, so I had to go see."

"Damn."

Zander whipped the wrench at Steve. "Shut the fuck up, man. You're reading way too much into this."

"Me thinks the gal who wasn't impressed with Zander Torris as a dinner date has stolen his heart."

"Me thinks my crew chief has been watching the goddamn TV too much." Zander wasn't mad, but his conversation with Steve had confirmed he'd hang himself if he answered questions about Molly to the media. The difference was respect. Maybe that was unfair and chauvinistic, but the women who basically threw themselves at him were getting exactly what they asked for when he used them as the flavor of the weekend.

"Hey, Z," called Josh, with Matt echoing him.

Zander grasped the hands of two other members of his pit crew using their team handshake and nodded. "Ready to tame this beast?" he gestured.

"You got it. Let me know if you need to kick some camera wielding, microphone toting ass," Matt said, casting a look toward the open door. They could see the line up of bodies along the fence, all vying for camera angles.

"Thanks, bud." Zander could count on his crew. They knew him, understood more than anyone how deep seated his hate for this constant personal scrutiny was. They also mirrored how dedicated Zander was to this sport, to each and every race, and ultimately, the championship. On race day, pussy didn't matter.

❧ ❧ ❧

"I can't accept this, can I?" Molly spoke out loud, not expecting an answer.

Angie, one of the counselors who had escaped to the air conditioning in the front offices snagged the paper out of her hand. Then squealed. "What do you mean, you can't accept this?"

"It just seems—"

"Hmmm, either he's thanking you for Wednesday night or he wants to see you again."

"Hmrph. Looks like a bribe to me."

"Molly! How can you think negatively? Fine. Take over for my cabin. I'm going." She fanned herself with the paper. "Oh my God. Zander Torris is such a hottie."

"Wait a minute."

Angie shook her short blonde hair and grinned. "I can't believe you'd even hesitate. I'm not even into racing and I'd be so there in a heartbeat. Get packing. Looks like your limo will be arriving in…holy crap, girl. Under an hour."

"I can't do that. Dr. Darrin isn't here, I haven't packed or checked out of my hotel room." Molly snagged her paper back and read it, then flicked a glance at her watch. Damn, Angie was right. This was going to be impossible. "I just can't—"

"Can't what?" Carl Browneberg, one of the directors, chose that moment to walk into earshot.

Before Molly could react, Angie had the fax paper again and was handing it to Carl. "Zander Torris just sent for Molly. Get Dr. Darrin here and tell Molly she needs to get back to her hotel and pack so she's not late for the limo."

"No." Molly walked around the counter and took possession of her itinerary. "I'm scheduled to be here until tomorrow afternoon."

"I've already talked to Team Transpro's representative about it, Molly. My wife's a retired nurse, and she's on her way to help Dr. Darrin for the next day."

Molly blinked. She never doubted Zander had connections, but there was still something amazing about watching strings get pulled before her very eyes.

"But the kids…"

"I'll be sure to tell them to watch for you on TV. Now you'd better get going if you want to see qualifying." Carl reached out for her hand. Molly obliged, despite the confusion that twisted in her stomach.

She was pissed, excited, confused and while she'd give anything to see Talladega, she'd donated her time to helping underprivileged kids, not support a millionaire race car driver.

"Go!" Angie laughed and gave her a playful shrug. "Wave to me on TV!"

"Are you—"

"I'm sure. You'll be coming back next year, right?" Carl's wide smile deepened his multitude of wrinkles.

"If you'll have me," Molly said. She couldn't stop staring at the single page of paper that was sending her world spinning.

"See you then."

It sunk in when she parked her car at the hotel and got out to a flash of white lights that rivaled a July Fourth fireworks display.

"What is the nature of the relationship—"

"What do you think of pictures taken yesterday of Mr. Torris and—"

"Are you going to the track—"

"Have the two of you kept this relationship under—"

Molly tried to ignore the leading questions that insinuated everything from Zander cheating on her to proposing she was "the other woman" or simply a good luck charm.

"Do you people have nothing better to do? What does it really matter who Zander's dating or seeing or having his pictures taken with? I'm a grown woman and watch enough TV to hear about Zander's reputation, which based on your talk, is based on about two percent truth and ninety-eight percent crap. So say what you will. Everyone knows it's fiction. You could have stayed home and written something up. Saved yourself and me a lot of time. Now, if you'll excuse me, I have a schedule to keep."

A fresh barrage of questions stopped her from talking. She tapped her foot and rolled her eyes. How did he do it? Yes, he'd been frustrated, but my God, these people were relentless!

"Listen," she toned down her temper. "Zander and I have one thing in common—the kids at the camp. If you want to report about something with a lot more heart than paper thin rumors, please see if you can drum up some donations for those kids."

Turning on her heels, she ignored their questions and clicked her cars remote alarm. She strode directly into the lobby of the hotel without looking back. Sort of felt like she had Wednesday night. Strange how things had changed, and yet stayed the same in just over a day.

"Miss Freibach?" called the desk clerk. After looking back and confirming the media mob squad hadn't followed her into the hotel, she walked up to the desk.

"I'm Molly."

"You have a limo arriving for you at ten-fifteen. Shall I buzz your room when he's arrived?"

She sighed. She was going to have to talk to Zander about this ordering her around stuff. If the prize wasn't to watch a race live at 'dega, she'd tell him to stuff it and head on home. "Thank you. I've got to hurry."

The clerk nodded, then smiled. What was with people and these half-smiles that made them look like they knew something she didn't? Did everyone around here listen to the news and believe all this buzz about her and Zander being an item?

Yet all the time she spent tossing items into her suitcase and carry-on duffle bag and double checking the hotel room to make sure nothing was left behind, she kept pinching herself.

By the time she had paced the room three times, checked the mirror several more, debating about changing, she was giddy with excitement. She told herself seeing Zander again was only part of her excitement. She'd be thrilled to go even if she had to sit in the nosebleed section off turn two and didn't get to talk to Zander. His final kiss had left her devastated but rethinking all those bad thoughts she'd had about him.

Her body hummed with an underlying tension she was afraid to define. He'd sent for her. Did that mean something beyond "I'm sorry for the hassle of the reporters"? She sighed, glancing at the phone, then her watch.

Heck with it. She was going downstairs to the lobby to wait.

The limo driver wasn't the least bit talkative. She rode in silence, not once entertaining thoughts of regret as he drove out of civilization and turned in a long drive that ultimately led to a small airstrip. But the Team Transpro and Kniola Automotive logos adorning the side of the Learjet parked arrogantly across the center of the field stole her unease, but made her tremble with anticipation. She was going to ride in the private team jet. Likely the same one Zander had ridden back to the track the day before.

"Thank you so much." She accepted her luggage from the limo driver and shook his hand. A man stood at the steps leading up into the jet.

Each step closer she got, the more confident she felt. Surely Zander hadn't gone through all this trouble just to say he was sorry. He would have just sent tickets, not arranged, that is, asked for someone to arrange for escort her all the way there.

"Good morning, Miss Freibach," the pilot said as he took her luggage from her.

"Call me Molly." Royalty sure had it made, 'cause she felt like a million bucks climbing those narrow steps and then stepping into the plane.

It wasn't quite as posh as she expected, but it sure beat the commercial flights she'd taken. The captain's chairs were sparsely placed, allowing plenty of legroom, and for one to recline nearly all the way.

She picked a seat near the window on the right side and sat down. Shame she hadn't packed a camera. Her dad and friends back home would love to see this. Molly Freibach sitting in Zander Torris's private jet!

"This is for you," said her pilot, who introduced himself as Wesley. "Let's get this bird off the ground."

She nodded, still stuck with awe. This was happening. She glanced at the envelope he'd handed her. Unwilling to wait, she withdrew the paperwork. Pit pass. Garage pass. Oh God. She'd be framing that when this was over. A note that said he was trying to firm up hotel reservations and apologized he couldn't get accommodations for her at the track. *Please.* As if she expected that.

She looped the ticket information, already tucked neatly into a plastic badge holder, around her neck. Glancing out the window, she vowed to have fun no matter what, because there was no way she'd ever get this opportunity again in her lifetime.

Chapter Five

"He's got it bad."

Steve Tanner jerked up, damn near hitting his head on the decklid of the race car. "What are you doing here?" he demanded of his wife.

Selma smiled and circled around her husband, her hands tracing over his hips. "I got bored in the motorhome. You know I'd rather be out here anyway. I just talked to Zander. Guess he caught some radio interview with Molly. Is that her name? Molly?"

Steve nodded and put down the wrench he was using to test the tightness of the fuel line connectors. "C'mere you. You're not matchmaking again, are you?"

Selma giggled as he tugged her against him. "I don't have to. He's got himself in this pickle all by hisself. You should see how pissed off he got. And that was when he was telling me about what he'd heard. I bet that radio is in pieces somewhere, knowing his temper."

Maybe there was something to the rumors, the reason the media had bit into this one like a pit bull on fresh meat. Zander had been moody all day yesterday. Not sullen, focused, just moody. Smiling one moment and ready to tear the sun from the sky the next. "I think you might be right."

"You need this race, don't you?"

His wife knew the ins and outs of the point racing better than most drivers. While she didn't officially work for the team, her presence was a common one in the garage, usually teasing the men, doling out encouragement and of course, dong a little matchmaking when he'd let her get away with it.

"A DNF will put us out of the top ten in points. That's a deficit I don't want to have to fight back from, not this close to the Chase cut off."

"I think I can help make sure he finishes—and finishes well."

"Honey, it's Talladega. Lady Luck is the only one who chooses the winner this week."

"And this week we'll name Lady Luck Molly. She's on her way to the track as we speak. Once he knows she's here, he'll do everything in her power to impress her. Guarantee it."

"But you'll be buried in the infield 'cause Zander will chop you in little pieces for suggesting you put Molly in front of the media again."

Selma laughed, her entire body vibrating against the front of him. Damn vixen. Yet she was brilliant. Clever.

"So?" she challenged. "He had a bag of her clothes he asked me to return. I had everything I needed to make it all happen and he doesn't suspect a thing."

Did he mention she was the bravest person he knew? He simply shrugged at her, knowing any warning he came up with would fly over her head.

"Then kiss me, stupid. I've still got some final arrangements to make."

"Get her a garage pass. Once he knows she's here, he'll insist she be here where he can keep tabs on her."

"Who?"

They both whirled at Zander's voice.

Selma snuggled closer to Steve. "Oh, I was thinking of calling Tess and seeing if she'll come to the track this weekend. I could use the company and I think Matt's over being an ass, don't you?"

Steve winced. Tess was a handful, and perfect for Matt. Sadly, Matt had a lot of growing up to do before he was ready to handle the likes of her. The last time they'd gotten together, the fireworks were intense. No one could forget it. But then Matt went and screwed it up by saying something about women not belonging in the sport.

Tess was a helluva racer, cremating the snot out of the competitors in the late model and dash series races all over the Carolinas. His wife was a genius, bringing her name up.

Zander groaned, as expected. "Matt would kick your tail," he warned, walking around his car. "She ready to run?"

"I'd rather walk, thanks," Selma commented.

Zander snorted. "I was talking to your husband, my dear. I'm just hoping you let him finish his job on my car here before you drag him back into your coach for the night."

"Not for the night…just an afternoon—"

"You lucky bastard," Zander quipped, picking up Steve's abandoned wrench. "Get out of here."

Selma's laughter echoed through the garage. For the next two days the garage would be packed with wall-to-wall people. Mechanics, sponsors, owners, drivers, all doing their part to get a car ready to visit victory lane.

Zander was looking forward to it. Not that he hadn't had plenty to do. Sponsor breakfast. Final practice. Press meeting. Thank God personal questions hadn't been allowed there because he had not been in the best frame of mind. Damn bastards had followed Molly and were hounding her. If her name had come up in the interview he might have been dragged out in handcuffs. Soon after that he'd found Pete and demanded he keep the media, except the reputable TV and radio network people, away from him.

"You're looking pretty sullen," Matt said, rounding the front of the car. It was nearly time to roll the car out for pre-qualifying inspection.

"Just had to chase Steve and Selma out of here. If my car had a backseat, they would have been in it."

"Ah, jealous, are you?"

Zander lifted an eyebrow. "Jealous?" That was new, no one had ever accused him of being jealous of anyone else's sex life.

"Where's your repertoire of trophy girls, Z?"

"Sent 'em home to their mommies. Way too much shit to do today. I still haven't gotten to review the notes. I wish they'd stop changing the rules. Spoiler's different than last year, the grill opening's changed. Damn, I'd feel better about this if we'd practiced here."

"Hello in there? Who's stolen Zander's body?" Matt leaned against the fender, then leapt off when Zander threatened to snap him with a shop towel.

"Get off there, ya punk. You know how aerosensitive those fenders are!"

"Yo, Z, chill, and yes, I do."

Zander pulled a deep breath. The knot at the base of his neck made the hunchback of Notre Dame's problem look minor. His stomach churned, but dammit, it hadn't been calm since he'd heard Molly's name on the radio earlier.

He wasn't mad at her. Just the opposite. If he wasn't so goddamn pissed at the bottom feeding reporters for following her around, he'd be proud of the way she dealt it to 'em. Still, handle it or not, it was his fault. He regretted pulling her into this even more. More so because as soon as he'd heard her voice he'd felt something. Desire, sure. His cock went semi-rigid every time he thought of her. But there'd been something more, something in the way she treated him Wednesday night as if he were simply a man, not some heroic race car driver. Then she'd put on that dress and he'd quit thinking.

By some grace of God he'd had the ability to walk away. Now he wasn't sure if that had made it better or worse.

"Let's get this car rolled out." Matt waved to the rest of the crew and smiled at Zander. "Take it out on the track, my friend, 'Cause this is 'dega."

Routine was good. Zander left the short pre-qualifying meeting psyched to do this. He loved this track, its wide back stretch and banked, sweeping corners. It was an all-out sort of experience, one in which control is an illusion. The car would top two hundred miles per hour and it would be up to him to steer it around the track.

He pressed the earpiece into his ear and then pulled his helmet over his head. Routine. He tested his belts, then his neck restraint. For the short qualifying runs, he wouldn't have the cool air vent hooked to his helmet—the only form of air conditioning in these race cars. But Sunday he'd be checking that too. Next the steering wheel went on, locked and checked. Then radio check. "Steve, you copy?"

"Gotcha, Z."

"Out."

He shrugged his shoulders, the small amount he could considering the tight quarters. Gloves were next. He shook his hands, wrapped his fingers around the steering wheel to make sure there were no constraints against movement. It was time to go. Time to get his game on.

"Whenever you're ready, champ. Seventeen's coming around for checkers in half a lap. Fire 'er up."

Zander reached out and flipped the toggle switches, holding and releasing the final one, the one that sent air, fuel and fire to work under the hood. The roar was nearly deafening inside the car, the vibration immediately rumbling as if the car were battered by the hooves of a team of skittish horses, just waiting to be unleashed.

"Roll, man, start to roll. Get those tires warmed up on the first lap. Side to side, side to side. Keep out of those marbles up there."

Hitting the pieces of rubber he alluded to could mean the difference between the pole and taking a provisional starting position. It was part of the routine.

"I got a good feeling about today." He spoke into the headset as he pressed the small button on the steering wheel to talk to his crew. "We're gonna get the pole."

"You can do it, Z."

He loved Talladega. This track with its curves and lack of inhibitions was a better lover than any woman he'd ever known. Yet when scorned, her bite was worse than a viper's, and damn near always as fatal. So far, he'd been lucky. He'd only known the exuberance of pushing the pedal all the way down and holding it there as he negotiated the high-banked curves. Almost to the wall, inches, sometimes fractions of inches as he took the corner, then swept to the middle of the track in the backstretch, holding his breath at the vision of the stands sweeping by in a blur of color. There were no speedometers in their vehicles, but he knew the car pushed two hundred on that long stretch of pavement. He loved qualifying. The track was his. Every inch, every mile. His to tame, his to race.

"Green flag, Torris. Hammer down."

At Talladega and Daytona it took a lap or two for the cars to come up to full speed. When he passed under the flag stand, his car was finally hitting peak speed. Tunnel vision took over, blinding him. He was barely aware of the g-force that tugged at his body inside the car. He forgot about the stands, the fans, pit road. All that mattered was the track before him and the feel of his car as it sliced through the air.

"Fifty-eighty-two," Steve called out. "A hair off the pole. Dig a little deeper for this final lap."

"I'm pushing."

"You want to impress Molly, don't you?"

His body went cold. Molly? Instinct powered that car around the second corner and swept into the backstretch for the final time. He blinked, digging within himself for the focus he needed to shave those few tenths of a second off his time. *Goddammit, Steve.* He was going to kick his ass right off the pit box when he got back to pit road. He knew better than to distract him like that.

Gritting his teeth, he flexed first one hand, then the other on the steering wheel and let momentum pull the car up the hill and around the final two corners. The bottom was the shortest distance around, but if he came off high and cut down low, gravity might give him a little more power. If he didn't sheer the tires too much or bottom out the front end.

"Seventy-two. Zander, you did it—that's the pole!"

Normally he would have whooped and hollered with Steve as she circled the track at a slower speed to catch the entrance to pit road in turn four. But when Steve had cued his mike to give him results, he'd heard her. At least he thought it was her. Definitely a female voice. Right there. Right next to Steve. Screaming. Selma had never done that.

And never had a woman's voice taken his insides and turned them into knots. He couldn't get back to pit lane fast enough, sliding his tires to a stop where the official indicated.

Shit. The media were already standing there, waiting for him. He prayed it was the TV guys only.

"Zander, great run. What gave you the extra boost—"

He'd been through this before, knew the questions and answered automatically while looking away when he could, searching for Steve or any other member of his crew.

At the first opportunity, he ducked away from the reporters and jogged over to the pit road area where Steve had timed his qualifying run. Nothing.

"Looking for someone?" Josh smiled and lifted one eyebrow.

"Yeah, where's Tanner?"

"Garage, of course. He's giving a tour."

"Tour?" Zander swallowed. Who would Steve be giving a tour to unless…

"You sly bastard. Damn fine job you did out there. We're gonna have to bring her to all the tracks."

"She's here?" He knew the question sounded flat, but he couldn't believe it. What the hell was she doing here? In Alabama…in his garage? He started toward the garage stall, but Josh grabbed his firesuit and stopped him.

"You can't go back there. Stay with the car, dude. Keep your head on."

Zander ground his teeth and shook his head. Josh was right. He'd be called upon to talk to the media if anyone knocked him off the pole or even came close. And if no one did, he'd be stuck up here for hours, doing photo shoots and interviews. Damn it.

. . .

"I'm sorry you didn't get the pole," Molly said as she walked up behind him.

Zander squinted up at the scoring tower, which listed his number in second place. "There'll be other chances."

She nodded, studying him. She'd seen him dozens of times in his firesuit, but somehow, standing here, this close, made it all so real. She'd had to pinch herself several times since arriving. Steve and Selma had greeted her. She'd known Steve from the television broadcasts, but hadn't expected him to be so down-to-earth and welcoming. His wife was amazing, a powerhouse of energy with a gleam in her eye. Made her wonder what Zander had told her, but as Selma grabbed her luggage and loaded it on the golf cart blazoned with the Team Transpro logo, Molly found herself answering questions she would have normally considered too personal.

Zander swallowed and looked at everything but her. She frowned. Did he have second thoughts? Maybe he was more upset than he was letting on about missing the pole. It had been a ridiculously tiny margin. And she wasn't a fool. It paid to win the pole.

"Steve gave you a tour already?"

She shouldn't have come. His tone was curt, short, disinterested. As if he was looking for a way to ditch her. Maybe he'd been guilted into sending her tickets. Maybe he hadn't done it. The thought curdled in her stomach, yet she knew it to be true. It was spelled out in the panic and confusion on his face. He hadn't expected her to be here and didn't know what to do with her. Pasting a smile on her face, she looked up at him and said, "I really want to thank you for inviting me. I'm so excited to be here. This is incredible."

God, was it hard to act thrilled when the creases in his forehead deepened and his dark eyes met hers. She knew this was too good to be true. Why…why…why! Did she let herself get her hopes up?

"Oh, good, she found you!" Selma slid her arm through Zander's and steered him back toward the garage area. "Let's get off pit road or someone's going to figure out who you are." She grinned at Molly, who'd fallen in step beside her. "You're practically a celebrity now."

Zander hissed, but didn't say anything. Molly wanted to laugh evilly at the way he looked like a petulant child with his mother leading him, humiliating him, away from the playground. Served him right.

"I put Molly's luggage just inside your trailer. She nearly missed qualifying."

"Fine," he practically barked.

"Maybe we should go get it and I'll head on to the hotel now. I don't want to be in the way." Coward's way out, but Molly knew when she wasn't wanted.

"Don't be ridiculous! There's all kinds of things going on here at the track tonight," Selma said, then slid her arm through Molly's as if to keep her from leaving.

While she would love to stay and experience this side of the life, she was beginning to feel more and more unwelcome the longer Zander's silence stretched on.

"I think it's supposed to rain." He finally offered.

"Oh quit being a scrooge, dammit. There's a barbeque, some of the guys were talking about a guys versus girls card game and—"

"We've got work to do."

Molly couldn't get any lower. There wasn't a scrap of doubt in her mind now—Zander didn't invite her and had no idea she was coming. And from the looks of it—he didn't want her here.

"I've already asked Steve. The car's perfect. There's nothing to be done except change the tires so you can scuff a few sets tomorrow during practice and see who you draft well with. The crew have had a few tough weeks, he's giving them the night off."

Molly glanced up at Zander as he flexed his jaw, the muscles there rippling. He stared straight ahead, but it was crystal clear he'd heard what Selma just said.

Was she that appalling?

"Get her out of here," he cut into Selma's next sentence. He jerked free and approached the guy walking toward them with a tape recorder.

"Let's go," Selma hissed. "Lord, don't piss him off any more. Keep your head down and follow me."

Molly was surprised they didn't run, but it's not like they were alone in the garage area. There were team members, pit crews milling about, talking racing, and talking life. It was overhearing those snatches of conversation that made her smile. Damn shame Zander was being such a stick in the mud. She'd like him to open up to her the way he had to that little boy at camp. Maybe she could find out what he was trying to prove here with this obsession with the media—and why. Lord knows these other race drivers didn't seem to be looking over their shoulders every two minutes.

"Now you've done it," Zander hissed to Selma when he caught up with them moments later. His eyes were black. Molly swore she saw flashes of lightning in them, then wondered if it was some tabloid's camera flash reflected there. His features had hardened, his cheekbones and lines of his jaw looks carved from steel. Thank God he was talking to Selma, 'cause she'd be shaking if he talked to her that way.

"You're so overdramatic about this," Selma retorted.

Molly felt her mouth fall open. She was taunting him! And did it without her husband around to protect her.

Yet Zander didn't seem surprised by her egging. "They know she's here. Now I've got to find someone to play fucking bodyguard for her or she'll never get a moment's rest. Neither will I."

"That's 'cause you bring it upon yourself. If you ignored them, they'd get bored and go pick on someone else."

They were away from the main throng of people and nearing the gated area where the driver's coaches were parked. "Where's your husband?" Zander demanded.

Selma shrugged. "I'm not his keeper."

"He should be yours, by God. You've meddled enough. I'm going to take Molly back to my coach and see if I can apologize enough for both of us. This weekend is going to be a nightmare for her. Why? Why did you do this?"

Selma winked at Molly, blew Zander a kiss and flounced away. Out of the corner of her eye, Molly could see Zander's hands tightening into fists. At any moment steam would blow out of his ears.

She wasn't dumb. Selma had been behind all of this, probably in some matchmaking effort. She understood that, didn't like being manipulated that way, but she didn't think the woman meant anything bad by it. In fact, she was pretty sure Selma Tanner didn't have a mean bone in her body. She also understood Zander's side. There was no denying the media's love affair with all things Zander Torris, and she'd be yanked right into the thick of things. And he was just chivalrous enough to play vigilant protector and make sure they never had the chance to ask her even one question. A lot of stress when he was "on the job".

She mulled her options as he cleared her through the guards at the gate and led her to his coach. "Listen," she said finally. Enough really was enough. She was an adult and being treated like a child was starting to piss her off.

Zander kept walking.

"Listen," she said louder.

Still didn't stop.

"Zander Torris, I'll yell what I've got to say loud enough for every damn reporter in this joint to hear me. I don't care, but I'm not gonna let you treat me like some pesky child just because—put me down! Dammit, Zander. Put. Me. Down." How dare he? He'd taken three giant strides and had her up over his shoulder as if she weighed nothing. Her ribs ached from bouncing with each step. She could barely speak, because the air was too quickly forced out of her lungs. He had a strong arm over her legs, so kicking would be useless. It was highly unlikely her fists pounding against his back would stop this determined march.

"I'm sure that will look good in the papers," she hissed at him when he finally put her down near the steps to his coach. He opened the door, practically tossed her inside and followed her in.

"Not my fault." He rubbed both his hands over his face, paced the length of the hallway and returned to her. "I don't blame this on you at all, but by God, you have no idea what you've gotten yourself into."

"Unlike you, I'm not afraid of the media. And I came on the pretense you sent for me. I'll be happy to leave on those same grounds." She reached for her suitcases, which were sitting on the sofa just inside the door. "Thanks. It's been fun." She tried to brush past him, but his looming form and the narrow hallways left her trapped and at his mercy.

"You..." He stepped closer. "Aren't going anywhere."

He put his hands on either side of her face and lowered his mouth to hers.

Chapter Six

Molly tried to back away. She took one step and the back of her knees collided with something, some sort of furniture, and she tottered backwards. Instinctively she dropped the suitcases and reached forward and fisted the material of Zander's firesuit. She kept from falling, but found herself even closer to the dangerous man who made thinking impossible.

No, thinking *was* possible, and with each movement of his lips against hers, each gentle stroke of his hot, velvety tongue over hers, her mind went wild. Zander hadn't said he was unhappy to see her, just that he wasn't happy she was here, within target of the media. He hadn't told Selma, at least while she was within earshot, that he didn't like Molly. In fact, he had to have said or done *something* to make Selma go through all the hassle of getting her here undetected.

Perhaps that spark of hope hadn't gone out yet.

His fingers tightened in her hair. The slight tinge of pain caused by his dominant possession sent shivers through her body. She really was limp in his arms, and there was no way to deny she was enjoying every moment of it. His mouth was amazing. His kisses were slow, the pressure just enough to awaken every nerve in her body—but especially those at the peaks of her breasts and between her thighs.

When his thumb grazed over her cheekbone, those fleeting thoughts faded. Her entire body trembled beneath the velvety touch. Every part of her body hummed in anticipation of knowing the magic of his fingers.

No hurry, despite the desperation she sensed. Was he feeling what she felt—the sensation of drowning with pleasure? If this was what it felt like to kiss him, how could she survive anything else?

A moan escaped her, one she wished she could immediately take back. It must have caused him to remember where he was, who he was with, because he let go of her immediately. If she hadn't been holding on to him, she would have fallen. As it was, she took a step back to catch her balance.

She expected him to apologize. Or blame her. Or grab her suitcases and escort her to the hotel himself.

But nothing about Zander Torris was predictable. He picked up the cases and carried them to the back of the coach. She couldn't see the room there but would have put money on it being his bedroom. A shiver of anticipation raced through her body as she understood—at least guessed—what that meant. When he came back, he had his driver suit peeled off his shoulders and the arms tied loosely around his waist. He wore a white racer shirt with mock turtleneck collar. Tight fitting material stretched over his muscular chest. Damn.

He'd looked awful good in a tux, but this was...*gawd*. She knew he watched her drink him in, but she couldn't tear her eyes from him. He crossed his arms over his chest. That just made it worse. She wanted to run her hands over the bulge of his biceps and feel the steely strength beneath the velvety tan skin.

"You're not helping me here," he said finally. Molly's knees went weak with the deep timbre of his voice. It reminded her of his parting comment in her hotel room. Christ, that seemed like years ago.

She lifted her eyes, deliberately slow. "Helping what?"

"Keep my sanity."

That, she decided, was the most promising thing he'd said yet. "So what are you going to do with me?" She hadn't meant it to sound like that, but didn't flinch when the words sank in.

"Lock you in here until it's time to go."

"Lock me in here?" Flirting with disaster, that's what she was doing. He stood there, as if daring her to take a step closer. "Alone?"

"Are you alone now?"

She smiled.

That's all it took.

Why she was here, what she'd think about her actions tomorrow or next week—none of that really mattered. She shouldn't be here, wasn't sure she'd do it again given the opportunity, but she wasn't able to help herself. Zander's kisses made her feel like she'd never been kissed before, his touch the first that set her skin on fire, yet made her want him to never stop touching her.

His mouth was less forgiving and more demanding this time, matching the darkened shadows on his face and determined midnight of his eyes. He was dangerous. She shivered as she read the desire on his face. For her. He wanted her. How, why, she didn't question, yet she knew. It was in the way he kissed her, drawing his tongue into her mouth and suckling, the grip his hand had on her arms. There's no way she would have gotten out of his grasp even if she wanted to. And no way did she want to right now.

His lips left hers and traced a path along her jawline and down her neck. Her body trembled as he found her erogenous zone along her pulse line. Electricity shot through her body, ultra-sensitizing her skin, igniting her blood. Muscles failed, breathing became an effort.

This man was a drug, pure and simple. She was high on the feelings no man had ever evoked in her before.

Before she even realized he'd released her arms, Zander scooped her up and carried her to the back of motorcoach. She giggled when he had to step sideways through the narrow galley walkway, and still managed to bump his head on the side cabinets. He just shot her a dark look she interpreted to mean nothing was going to stop him.

The bedroom—more of a king-sized bed surrounded by walls—was amazing. The closet doors were mirrored, a fact that both made her nervous and excited her. She had never felt small, but seeing the reflection of Zander holding her, she felt petite and feminine. With her face flushed and lips swollen and pink from his kisses, she actually *looked* sexy.

That shot a spark of awareness through her body. It was like reality hitting. Zander Torris. *The* Zander Torris wanted her. And from the looks of it, was going to have her.

"Beautiful," he whispered, the scruff of his unshaven cheek grazing her neck. She squirmed and clenched her thighs together, still amazed at how quickly her body responded to his sensuality.

She met his eyes in the mirror. The darkness there faded, leaving a luminescence that bore straight through to her heart. Her chest tightened. No, she wasn't a fool. Letting her emotions get involved, at least more involved, would be certain heartbreak.

"Kiss me again," she demanded, needing to chase such thoughts away.

"You kiss me." He laid her on the bed and loomed over her. She backed up over the lush, dark comforter as he climbed onto the bed between her feet and crawled up toward her.

When he was nearly over her, she grabbed his face between her palms and pulled his face down to hers.

He crushed her. Groaning, he thrust his tongue into her parted lips. She gave in to the pressure on her thighs and opened them to him willingly. As his tongue stroked hers, he lowered his hips to hers, pressing his hard-on against her swollen clit.

She moaned and lifted her hips. Too many layers of clothing separated them, yet the friction of his weight and movement against her was erotic as hell. His tongue was magic, sweeping over her parted lips, then diving inside. Coupled with the sweet pressure against her aching pussy, it was all she could do not to die from the pleasure.

Molly was breathless when he straightened himself over her and looked down. Only the most intimate part of their bodies touched. She reached up, realizing her hands were free. How could she not be touching, exploring…removing clothes!

But when she placed her palm over Zander's stomach and the muscles there jumped, the rush to undress him turned into a need to feel every crevice and bulge, every muscle, sinew, and inch of flesh.

Half-dizzy from the constant shifting of pressure against her clit, she watched her fingers trace over the outline of his muscular abs through his snug shirt. Feeling his body react was such a rush. She stroked his ribs, then followed the lines of the shirt up to his shoulders, then over the well formed muscles of his upper arms. This man was built like a dream.

She tugged at his shirt, pulling it free and slipping her hands beneath it. When she brushed his hot skin, he shuddered. She gasped, amazed she could evoke such reaction in him. His body was tight, truly that of an athlete. The need to see him bare-chested won over the enjoyment of torturing him with the light grazes of her fingers down his ribs and over the downy soft trail of hair that led south from his navel.

Eventually she wanted to taste him, to kiss the hard plain of his stomach and follow the line.

Treasure trail. Yep, there was a reason they called it that.

"You worry me when you smile like that."

She lifted her face to meet his eyes. "I worry *you?*" She could hardly believe that. While she hated to think about it, she knew this man had been with his share of women. Her experience would be somewhere in the novice category in comparison.

"You do," he answered, bending his arms and lowering his mouth until it nearly touched hers. His breath tickled her flesh, her body humming in anticipation of his kiss. Yet he paused there, holding himself up for an impossibly long time, teasing her with the minimal space separating their bodies.

"Zander," she whispered, reaching up to say his name again, against his lips.

"I take that back." He devoured her with his hungry kisses. "You don't worry me. You excite me. I can't decide whether to kiss you all over or get those damn clothes out of the way and bury myself inside you."

Those words woke another level of passion inside her, one which wanted that too. Wanted it a little hard, a little rougher than their cautious exploration had been so far. His admission had stolen her ability to form words. Her body screamed for attention. Skin on skin, his cock filling her intimately, driving, pushing, racing to the edge and back. Moaning, she pushed him upward until he once again held his weight on those python-like arms. Licking her lips, Molly reached between them and tugged at the waistband of his firesuit, releasing the loosely tied sleeves and then shoving the thick material out of her way.

Her mouth went dry when she saw what he wore beneath them. Snug, gray boxer briefs hugged his narrow hips and sexy ass. His thick cock was clearly outlined, evidence that his desire matched hers. Her body tensed, her intimate muscles flexing as she anticipated how he would press into her, stretching her, filling her. Her hips bucked with the mental images, and he complied, pressing his length against her.

She moaned and dug her fingers into his back, pressing him as close as she could.

Zander rocked against her, his cock as hard as steel. His control seemed to be slipping. His eyes were squeezed closed, his breathing nearly as erratic as hers as he moved against her.

She moaned, tensing as he applied pressure at just the right spot and pushed her closer to the brink. God, she needed him, wanted him. Not like this—she wanted more. Fisting his shirt, she tugged upward, trying to convey her need to get the pesky clothes out of the way. Now. There'd been enough teasing.

He understood and lowered himself to the bed beside her, still touching her. Instead of removing the rest of his clothing, however, he reached for the button of her jeans and loosened it with a flick of his fingers. The sound and vibration as he lowered her zipper was torturous. She nearly swore as he slipped his hand between the thick denim and her cotton panties and stroked her pussy.

She wriggled her hips, both because his fingers turned a bonfire into an inferno and she was about to combust, but because she needed those damn jeans out of the way. She wanted him inside her when she came, and then if he wanted to make her come again...and again. She gasped at the mental image of the ways she wanted to fuck Zander.

"Get these off," she hissed, finally finding her voice. Tugging at his shirt again, whimpering, she said, "This too."

His fingers receded, leaving her breathless. He sat up and kicked off his shoes, removing the rest of his uniform and finally pulling that damn shirt over his head. She followed suit, more than unwilling to wait to let him work his way down her body. She'd never survive.

"Wait, let me look," he growled when she'd removed her shirt and reached for her bra closure. His voice vibrated through her as if he'd touched her everywhere at once. She knew she was trembling. All he had to do was speak, or reach for her and she'd surrender everything to him. From the unguarded look of lust on his face, she didn't think he was holding back either.

"You're beautiful," he said.

Her body quivered, her breasts aching for his touch as he reached for them. She arched into him, offering herself as he closed his palms over her. It felt so good, the way he possessed her. He kneaded her flesh, finding her nipples and pinching through the lacy material of her bra. Spirals of electricity pooled between her thighs with each tug or graze across the tightened peaks of her breasts. Was it possible to climax from just this? She'd bet on it.

Molly popped the snap and tossed her bra to the foot of the bed with the rest of her clothes. She watched him as he drank her in, feeling self-conscious, that nagging little thought of knowing she likely didn't measure up to those physically perfect trophy girls who walked around the garage and had probably ended up here a time or two.

But she saw no sign of disappointment, or distraction, in Zander's darkened gaze, and forced herself to take this moment for what it was. He wanted her. Lord knows she wanted him and would die if he didn't give her an orgasm—soon.

"Zander!" she cried out when he lowered his head to her breast and suckled. The sensations that shot through her body, curling her toes, stealing her breath, dampening her panties even more—were incredible. He pressed his tongue to her nipple, then gently tugged with his teeth before shifting his weight and starting over with the other.

She slid her hands into his thick hair, noting that even the sensation of the dark waves against her fingers was exaggerated and erotic. This man was sensual, sexual and capable driving her insane, yet pleasuring her to the limit.

He ignored her attempts to nudge him upward, at this point, she was nearly willing to push him on his back and take what she wanted herself. She almost laughed, wondering what he'd say about that. He'd definitely taken the driver's seat on this one, but the idea of wielding power over Zander Torris had a definite appeal.

It wasn't happening right now. He had her too weak to fight him, too close to the edge to dare stop anything he offered. She bit her lip and moaned as he lowered one hand to her cup her pussy, rocking his hand over her mound as he suckled her breast.

"I want—" she couldn't say it. She'd never ordered a man to fuck her before, yet if she didn't make him do it now, she'd shatter into a million pieces before he got inside her.

His lips left her breast and traveled up until they tickled her collarbone. The nibbles he placed there were no less erotic than the feel of his mouth on her now-aching breasts. "Want what, sweetheart?"

"You." It came out as a pant. The full length of his body pressed against hers, that rock hard cock stabbing against her thigh. Her pussy quivered at the thought of him guiding himself to her opening and pressing into her tightness. She damn near cried with the need to feel him.

He must have read it on her face or heard it in her voice. He grabbed the front of her panties and tugged. She lifted her hips, facilitating the removal, but she had no doubt he'd tear them from her if he had to. His shorts melted off somehow, she didn't even notice him shift to remove them. She heard a rustle. Condom. Thank God one of them was thinking.

God, she could come just from the dangerous, shadowed look on his face. It was damn near animalistic, something primitive. Her chest felt like it was going to burst. His eyes bore into hers. She couldn't breathe, couldn't think, just watched as this gorgeous man lowered his body to hers.

His lips captured hers once again, the heat and pressure searing her mind closed of anything except this moment. Her nipples tightened, painfully rubbing against the hairs that darkened his chest. But his cock, oh God, it pressed against her thigh, just a hairsbreadth from where she needed him to be.

She tried to shift, did everything to get him to move, to find the place she knew he'd fit perfectly. She was ready. More than ready.

Yet he seemed satisfied devouring her mouth with his kisses, stroking his tongue against hers, teasing her with the motion and sensation that sent her head spinning. She pressed her nails into his back and arched against him, whimpering against his lips.

"You make me nuts," he said without withdrawing his mouth. But he shifted, eliciting a moan from her as the head of his engorged cock settled against her swollen slit. "Damn, you make me nuts."

She arched up, opening her mouth, her body, her very soul to him at that moment in exchange for the release she needed so badly. He answered, pushing inside her, stretching, shifting.

The power of this pleasure would kill her, she was sure of it. He withdrew slightly, leaving her desperately unfulfilled, but then surged forward again.

Her tight muscles relaxed, allowing him in. He buried himself to the hilt, dropping his head to her neck and pressing his face against her as he held her there, just for a moment before he started moving again.

This was bliss. Her body was no longer flesh and blood, but all feeling and sensation. Electricity hummed through every nerve ending. Blood pounded through her veins and her breaths were gasps. Nothing mattered except the friction of his cock against the walls of her pussy and the pressure of his body covering hers.

Each stroke was harder, faster. She met each one and begged for more. She heard him groan against her neck as he lifted his head and pushed himself up so he could see her.

Their eyes met. Something there, in the dark depths of his gaze hit her square in the chest. His pace increased. She arched her hips, taking him in, all of him, over and over again until she couldn't tell where she ended and he began.

"Z-Z-Zander," she gasped when the first of the power shocks ripped through her body with white-hot pleasure. She tried to keep her eyes locked with his, but the power of the orgasm that slammed into her with his very next, very deep stroke erased everything but the feel of him inside her.

She felt him let go, his body driving him in and out of her with an intensity that drew out the mind-numbing sensations that shook her physically and mentally. Then he stiffened, an indiscernible growl ripping from his throat as he pounded out his own release. She shuddered at the sensation of him throbbing inside her.

They lay there for a few minutes, their bodies still connected. Molly listened to Zander's uneven breathing and felt his ragged pulse against her chest. Whose heart beat faster, she wasn't sure.

This was the part she hated, the part where she didn't know what to say, what to do. What would Zander expect? Want?

Until he moved, she was more than content to lay there, the ultra soft comforter and mattress cushioning her from Zander's weight. Closing her eyes, she traced her fingers over his shoulder and down his side. What a fool she was. But an oh-so-blissfully satisfied one.

"Am I too heavy?" She barely heard him as he mumbled into the blanket.

"No." *You're perfect,* she wanted to say. And then encourage him to stay right here, where she could ignore the outside world for as long as possible and pretend they didn't come from such different lives. But that was a fantasy in which Zander actually cared for her for more than as a camp volunteer and now bedmate. Sex toy. Arm candy—hadn't he actually called her that?

She let out her breath and hated that she thought of it, here, now. Dammit.

"I'm moving, I'm moving." Zander half-slid, half-crawled off her, but only to snuggle beside her and wrap her in his arms.

Well, at least he had a good after sex manner. She could forgive the arm candy comment pretty easily with a few more minutes of this kind of treatment. A girl could almost fool herself into thinking she was living that fantasy.

Almost. Her fantasy wouldn't include annoying cell phones, but one was clearly present here.

"Don't answer it," he mumbled.

She laughed. "It's not mine, why would I answer it."

"Dammit."

She couldn't have answered it, because she couldn't even speak. Zander stood, over six feet of gorgeous manflesh, completely naked in front of her. Then he stretched! Muscles all over rippled and tightened as he reached up and grunted. Dayum. The awe-inspiring view continued as he stepped over their discarded clothing and walked into the hallway. His ass was fine. She normally only admired jean clad behinds when other women pointed them out and wasn't want to give a second glance to pictures of naked men, but this? She was practically drooling.

The tired yet sated feeling that kept her curled up on the comforter was because of that man. God hadn't spared any expense sculpting him. Regardless of what happened next, she vowed she would not regret this. Never.

"I've got to go." Zander walked back in looking rather defeated. "I'm sorry, Mol, but there's all these functions they demand I attend. I can't get out of them." He pulled his snug boxers back up, then yanked open the closet.

There was some satisfaction in the true apologetic tone in his voice and the way he pulled on the closet door. Still, he didn't say anything about her going, being by his side. She pulled her knees up to her chest and wrapped her arms around them, feeling very naked and exposed. She met his eyes in the mirrored door. "I suppose I'll head to my hotel then."

"No." He jerked a shirt out so hard she heard the hanger ping off the back of the closet and clatter to rest at the bottom. "This is your hotel."

Molly shook her head and took a deep breath. "I didn't come here to…fuck you, Zander." Make love just sounded too damn intimate, yet that's what it was for her. "I came to see the race, live the fan experience of Talladega. The pit pass, garage pass—all that's icing on the cake. A hotel would have been fine with me."

"You're staying here."

Batting her sudden shyness aside, she unfolded herself and reached for her clothes, forcing herself to dress as if it were the most common thing in the world. "I'm not a dog or a kid, Zander. You can't just order me around."

"The media are sharks."

"Been there, done that. They don't frighten me."

Zander buttoned the short sleeve denim shirt with his sponsor logo blazoned on the left chest and shot her a look that was supposed to intimidate her into staying. He probably was used to having to kick the women out, not beg them to stay. And she might have stayed, willingly even, if he wasn't so quick to treat her like a possession. "There's no way I will let you go to a hotel."

"I'm flattered, Zander, really I am, but you said it yourself, you have obligations. You didn't invite me here. I'm just in the way."

She lifted an eyebrow at his growl. Thing was, she really didn't want to leave—but knew she'd be compromising herself if she just gave in and let him order her around. That wasn't who she was. Neither was having sex with a man she barely knew, but there wasn't much she could do about that now, was there?

"There's your phone again." She finished dressing and grabbed her luggage. It really was all a bluff. No way would Zander let the guards let her out. No one would cooperate to call her a cab. Her original plan had included a hotel, but she doubted there had ever been reservations for her. Well, yeah, right here in Zander's trailer.

"Don't you dare move," he said as he stood in the narrow hallway, preventing any chance of her getting by. "You're not leaving."

She didn't bother to listen to him, instead attempted to smooth her hair in the mirror.

"What size do you wear?" Zander was back in the bedroom, his hand over the mouthpiece of the phone.

"Why?" She gave herself a mental high five. She really hadn't expected him to give in, but clearly he was doing just that—arranging for her to be with him.

"Just freaking tell me."

"Size for what? Jeans? Dress? Shirt?"

"Why do you women have to be so cockeyed complicated?"

"Jeans, six. Dress probably the same. Jeez, Zander, you had that dress all picked out the other night, I figured you knew everything about me already."

"Six," he said into the receiver, walking back out of the room.

She stuck her tongue out at him and sat down, waiting for him to come back with this evening's itinerary and to tell her a new wardrobe was on its way.

"You're going with Selma and some other wives to some charity thing. She'll be by with a sponsor shirt. I'm late."

He dropped a kiss on her anger-wrinkled forehead and walked out.

Molly followed. No way. No freaking way was he doing this to her. "Zander!" she cried, reaching for the handle and damn near breaking her fingertips off when the door refused to budge. "Torris!" she screamed, hoping the coach had poor insulation so everyone would know Zander had locked her in there. What an asshole.

She pried at the lock, but the door still didn't move. Oh, this was wrong. Totally wrong. Selma would agree with her. She'd make things right.

Chapter Seven

Zander didn't think the night would ever end. His mind had been back at the track—in the bed of his motorcoach to be exact—during the entire dinner. Several times Steve had kicked him under the table to keep up his end of the conversation.

His thoughts were locked on Molly. He'd pushed her, he knew. He just hoped Selma had enough determination on this bit of matchmaking to keep Molly from jumping ship and heading to a hotel room. God, he couldn't believe he actually formed those thoughts. The guys would never let him live it down if he admitted he *wanted* Selma's help here.

But Molly wasn't like the other girls. Not only because of who she was, but what she did to him internally. Sex with her had hit a chord somewhere and if he had his way, they'd still be in his bed discovering one another.

"Torris," Steve hissed at him.

"Get me out of here," Zander whispered back. "Obligations met."

"What's with you man, never seen you this screwed up over a girl?"

"It's not that," he insisted. "I can't believe we missed the pole today. I want to go over the notes for race day."

"Bullshit."

Zander lifted his water and gulped the cool liquid down. It did little to calm the fiery burn in his gut. *Admit it, Torris, you're afraid she'll leave you.*

He stood and leaned over the table, thanking the associate sponsor representative and turning down their offer for an after dinner drink.

Steve followed him out of the restaurant. "Dammit, Zander, you're being borderline rude."

"Get your wife on the phone and make sure she didn't let her leave."

"Who?"

Zander turned on him and frowned. "Don't give me that shit. I want her back at the motorcoach when I get there. Now, we going or should I just hail a cab?"

"Cab?" Steve snorted. "Get in the damn truck."

Zander cursed Steve under his breath when his friend blatantly laughed at him for getting out of the truck before it stopped. The lights were on in his coach, definitely a good sign. He didn't bother to bid Steve good night.

Molly met him at the door, arms folded over her chest. Only the flicker of amusement in her eyes gave her away. "You're lucky I like Selma."

"Really?" he asked, stepping up into the motorcoach and locking the door behind him. "I wanna watch."

"Zander!"

He loved it, her eyes were big as half dollars. Grinning, he nodded back toward the door. "If Selma's here, I'll go get Steve before he leaves and he can join in."

"No!" she gasped, backing up.

"No?" he repeated, stepping closer to her, effectively herding her toward the bedroom. Right where he wanted her.

"I-I-I—no."

"Never had a threesome, or foursome?" he teased, knowing damn good and well she hadn't.

"Um, I-I-"

"Me neither, and honey, I ain't sharing you with anyone. Even Selma, hot as that sounds."

"You bastard."

"You like me."

"I do?" She lifted an eyebrow.

"You're not going to a hotel."

"Oh please, as if you had given me any choice." She sat as the back of her knees hit the edge of the mattress. He stayed two steps from her, watching her fingers fiddle with the hem of her shirt. He understood little about women, but could tell she was nervous, and since she wasn't hostile, he could only guess it was because she was insecure.

"If I had let you leave, would you have?"

She stared at him a moment, then licked her lips.

He nearly groaned. His cock stirred to life at the gesture. "Well?"

"Depends."

He leaned against the wall, barely able to keep himself from closing the distance between them. She looked adorable in the pale blue T-shirt, the way it clung to her breasts and skimmed the top of her thighs. His chest tightened as he lifted his eyes back to her face and watched her expression as he asked, "Depends on what?"

"On why I should stay."

"Well, that's easy. I want you to."

She tightened her lips and shifted her weight. "Why?"

He glanced at the still wrinkled bed behind her, then back to her face. "I should say because the sex is great, but even before that I couldn't get you outta my head."

"Oh." She blinked, then looked down at her hands.

"Molly—"

"Shut up, Zander."

"I can do that." He took those final two steps and wrapped her into his arms. "I was afraid you'd left." Burying his face into her hair, he inhaled her scent. Something about her got under his skin.

"Afraid I'd leave? I'm in your way here." She pushed him back to look up at him. She searched his eyes, daring him to lie to her.

He couldn't, not even if he tried. He wanted to tell her the truth, it was admitting it to himself that was scaring the shit out of him. Molly Freibach had found her way into a part of him he thought he'd locked down tight. He didn't believe in love at first sight and doubted she'd believe him, heck, love seemed much too strong even for him at this venture. But there was something there, something that made him realize he didn't want her out of his sight—out of his arms.

"Don't say that. Don't you ever say that." He ran his hands down her arms, squeezing her fingers, then lifting them to his lips. He kissed her fingers, finding satisfaction in the way her shoulders relaxed and her lips parted with a sigh. When he was done, he placed her hands on his chest and covered them with hers. "Touch me, Molly. I promise I won't answer the phone this time."

She tilted her head and grinned up at him. "You can't ignore the phone."

"Okay, I won't answer it until tomorrow morning when I'm late for the hospitality tent."

She let out a laugh. God, she was beautiful when she smiled. Her whole face lit up, giving her a glow no amount of makeup could match.

"Why are you looking at me like that?" Her voice was soft, almost curious.

"I can't help it." He never understood women and was ready to accept the concept of them all having some magical power to steal a man's ability to think straight. He should be thinking cars, lap times and reviewing his promo schedule, not dreaming up all the wicked things he wanted to do to her body.

"So you want me to stay here so you can look at me?" she teased, tracing circles on his chest. Her eyes flickered downward, then back up to his.

He couldn't answer her. She devastated him with the innocent flirtation. He was a goner.

She sighed and melted against him as he brushed her lips with his. Her hands slid upward and encircled his neck, pulling his mouth down to hers. Their tongues tangled almost immediately, hungrily stroking each other.

When she shifted against him, pressing her stomach against his aching cock, he knew there would be no slow and easy with her—at least not yet. There was too much passion between them. His patience was being tested already and he hadn't gotten her undressed yet. The way she tugged at his buttons, he sensed the same urgency in her.

"Let's do this the smart way." He reluctantly pulled his mouth off hers and took a half step backwards. He lifted her hands from his shirt and made quick work of the buttons. "Get the clothes out of the way first."

She already had her shirt pulled over her head and reached for her bra strap. He paused to watch her remove the scrap of white lace.

Sweat broke out on his body. Her breasts were perfect. Not too big, not too small. As he looked at them, their peaks hardened into pink nubs he couldn't wait to get his mouth on. He'd never been much of a breast man, probably because there were too many plastic ones running around, but Molly just might convert him.

"Get undressed," she said, placing her hands over her nipples. "You're staring at me like you've never seen a naked woman before."

Her skin was flushed with her blush. Everything she did amazed him. Maybe because she was genuine. Maybe he needed to stop analyzing why and just accept it. He wasn't used to women like Molly. Women were arm candy or for physical release. Molly was for keeps.

Damn shame—terrible damn shame he wasn't the type of man who could keep a woman.

"You were pretty upset when I left, why the change of heart?" He nibbled his way down along her arm.

"Mmm, that hotel room would be pretty lonely."

He looked up at her without removing his mouth from her wrist. He knew Molly well enough to know it wasn't as simple as that. "And," he said, dropping kisses between his words, "so you were just looking for company? Why me?"

"No one else offered."

He laughed, then scooped her into his arms. She immediately wrapped her legs around his waist and locked her hands behind his neck. Her playful giggle was muffled against his shoulder. "Zander!"

"So if one of the other guys would have invited you to stay with them, would you have considered it?" he said. He'd intended to punish her, but it seemed he was suffering far more than she was right now. She was too busy laughing.

"No. Yes. Of course not, you dope."

He smiled, happy to hear her say it, even though he knew better. But he still didn't get the answer to his question. "Why aren't you destroying me for locking you in here?"

"Kiss me, dammit."

"Not until you tell me."

"'Cause you're cute." She had the advantage, again. He held her up, while she had her hands free. She placed her palms on his cheeks and tilted his head up for her light kiss. "Now, shhhh," she whispered against his lips. The vibration from the sound sent a shiver through his whole body.

Did it really matter why? She was here, more than willing to share his bed. Groaning, he opened his mouth to her prodding tongue and surrendered knowledge of anything else but Molly.

She was a tease. Her lips nipped at his lightly when he wanted a deep kiss, then left his mouth and traced along his jaw when he was willing to give in to her lighter, nibbling bites. It was frustrating as hell, especially when each time she shifted she rubbed against his cock. He looked around the room, wondering if he could simply press her up against the wall and show her exactly who was boss in here.

Just when he was ready to take her back out to the kitchenette area and sit her on the counter, she changed her mind about telling him. He growled in frustration when she wriggled free and sat on the edge of the bed.

"I'm not here because you're Zander Torris, even though if you weren't, I wouldn't be here, because—well, you know all that." She dropped her head to her hands, but not before he could see her blush.

He fisted his hands, if only to keep from closing the gap between them. His body was cold without the contact of her skin against his, yet something kept him back, some sense that told him she needed to say something before...

"I understand," he said. "I think."

She grinned up at him, her eyes sparkling. "I don't know you real well, but I like you. Not what you are, but who you are."

"That's fair enough, now can we—"

"Zander!"

He took a deep breath and folded his hands over his aching cock. Did this woman have any clue what she was doing to him? "C'mon." His voice was barely above a growl.

"Selma said you've never had another woman in your coach."

He shrugged. "I haven't."

"Then why me?"

"Ask Selma, she brought your stuff here."

"You could have gotten it and brought it back to me," she countered.

He knew exactly what she was asking, and he wasn't ready to answer it. How could he, without getting her hopes up? Last thing he wanted to do was break her heart. His, he could give a shit about, it was so scarred and torn, he was likely not to feel a thing when she returned to her life in Ohio and he went on to the next track.

"You know damn well you're not like any of the other girls."

"How? What makes me different?"

What indeed? This conversation was over. He couldn't spell out what made her different. Her background, her genuine personality, the richness of her attitude. The very fact she wasn't here because of his name or his money—yes, he believed her. That's what it was about Molly.

He knelt down on the floor in front of her and ran his hands up her legs. She watched him, her brows knit and head tilted when he kissed her knees, then slid his fingers up and down her calves.

His body responded to her surprised gasp when he nudged her knees apart and lowered his head to her inner thigh. There he pressed a kiss, nibbling just slightly with his lips as he traced back up to her knee before starting on the other leg. He could smell her. The sweet nectar of aroused pussy teased his nostrils. It was all he could do not to press her thighs apart and bury his tongue in her cunt, lapping her cream until she flooded his face with her come.

She'd probably like it, too.

Shit. His balls ached. Molly turned what had been a purely physical act of release into something emotional. His goal wasn't simply to elicit an orgasm from her and take one for himself, but to worship her body, to give her the best sex he could.

Man, he was losing it. Pussy never did this to him. Bad thing was, he already knew it wasn't pussy that did it. It was the woman attached to it who had gotten to his long dormant heart.

"Zzzander…" she hissed as his tongue grazed her swollen pussy lips. She opened her legs wider and leaned back on the bed, giving him access to her most sensitive spot. He accepted the invitation without hesitation, but still held back from feasting like a starving man. He watched her face as he ran his tongue up over the folds of her pussy, barely touching her.

Those little mews she made between gasps told him how effective his patience was. He repeated that move a few more times, applying a little more pressure at each pass. She pressed her hips upward toward him. He held her still. It was his turn to drive, and he intended to be there at the end of this endurance race.

Parting her lips with his hands, he found the sensitive nub of her clit and pressed his tongue there. She bucked under him, her fingers tugging at his hair as he refused to move. He did it again, tracing along the edges of her clit, then taking a long, slow lap upwards over that bud until she whimpered.

Moisture poured from her slit. He pressed his lips to it, tasting her tangy sweetness. His body tightened, his cock felt like it would split from the pressure, the need to be inside her, the hot wetness of her pussy clenching around him, eliciting every nerve to scream out.

Zander lifted his face for a minute and clenched his teeth. Control was fleeting. When she grabbed his hair and pressed his mouth back against her cunt, he gave up slow and easy.

He wrapped his arms around her thighs and nearly lifted her onto his tongue. He found her clit and vibrated his tongue against it, until her body shook with the force of her breathing. Then he suckled her hard nub until she cried out.

His mouth fucked her without apology, his tongue driving in and out of her slit, tasting, pressing, suckling there, then circling her clit until she squirmed and begged for release.

She was so fucking hot. He rocked his mouth back and forth over her as she gasped. He knew she was close. A few more hard rubs over her clit and she'd let go.

His intention had been to take her there this way, but his greedy cock wanted to feel her convulsing as she came.

He pulled her to her feet. She swayed and leaned against him. Her face was flushed, her eyes half closed and glassy. The entire time he fought with the damn condom, she pressed kisses to his chest and shoulder.

Sitting down on the bed, he pulled her onto his lap. Her wet cunt rubbed against the head of his cock. He groaned and reached down to guide himself inside her. Molly shifted, arching her back so he could deeply penetrate her hot, wet pussy. He grabbed her hips and held on, blinded by the sensations that rushed over him. They rocked together, moving only enough to create mind-numbing friction against his cock.

Her breasts pressed against his chest. If only he could touch her and kiss her all at once. The pain of her fingernails biting into the skin on his back only added to the pleasure. With each thrust, she moaned. He bit back his own groan, hoping to hold off his impending orgasm until she exploded on his cock.

When she lifted her eyes to his and smiled, he lost it. He dropped his lips to hers and met her mouth with a hard, demanding kiss as he held her hips tight and drove as deeply within her as he could. Her body shuddered around his. She bit down on his lip, the pain of her teeth spiraled straight to his cock. His hips ratcheted against hers, relentlessly until he felt her let go. The muscles of her cunt clamped down on his cock. He roared out her name against her lips as he came deep within her.

At that very moment he realized what he had done. He went rigid with fear and regret.

She seemed to not notice his withdrawal. She lay against him, her head cradled against his shoulder. He wrapped his arms around her and buried his face in her hair. He knew. Right then, right there. It was happening.

He'd gone and fallen in love.

Chapter Eight

Molly sat up in bed, careful not to wake Zander as she slipped from his loose grasp. She'd never fully fallen asleep, just some fitful state where her body relaxed and her mind went on and on and on. Even now, as she stared down at his face, so peaceful in sleep, she asked herself if it was worth it.

She was nothing to him, just another casual weekend fling. Yes, Selma had told her that as long as she'd been coming to the tracks, Zander had never brought a girl back to his private motorcoach. She had filled her with hope, excitement, and Molly had acted on it.

It wasn't the sex she regretted. It was opening her heart to him. But dammit, when he'd looked at her, his eyes all shadowy, she'd felt something, as if he were reaching out to her. She'd seen past all the machismo of his reputation, the allure of his fame and money and saw that same lonely man she'd gotten a glimpse of at the campground.

That was the man she'd surrendered herself to last night.

And that fantasy was so easy to believe right now, watching Zander's chest rise and fall, his much-too-long eyelashes brush his cheeks. She wanted to touch his lips, trace the outline of his ear, feel the scratch of his unshaven cheeks.

She swallowed and closed her eyes, then pulled her knees up to her chest and rested her chin there. Too much thinking. Why did she have to feel? Why couldn't she have an emotionless sex-filled weekend with the most tempting man she'd met yet? There was nothing she could think of to use as a rational excuse why she shouldn't do this, except the obvious. She'd end up falling for him and have her heart literally crushed when she saw him on television next week with two blonde trophy girls hanging off his arms.

"Whatsa matter?" he muttered, his arm snaking up over her legs and pulling her to him.

"Nothing," she whispered, smiling down at him. These were the moments she felt the most. Her heart damn near exploded from her chest with the power of it. She was insanely jealous of every other woman who'd witnessed this Zander, drowsy, sexy, like a giant tiger wanting to curl up for a catnap.

Even his growl, probably intended to mean he didn't believe her, struck a chord.

"Turn out the light," he muttered. "Get under covers."

He didn't open his eyes or move.

"Fine." She laughed softly at him. No doubt he'd be in the exact same spot when she got back. "I'll be right back."

She padded to the kitchen to turn off the light, and poured herself a tall glass of water while she was there. On the counter near the sink she spotted a prescription bottle.

Sleeping pills.

At first she frowned and looked back over her shoulder. Then she remembered Selma's words. She'd called Zander a lost soul and said he had displaced passion. From the few hours with her, she'd learned a lot about Zander, and realized how little of it surprised her.

He was a loner, not allowing anyone close to him—just a few crew members and his car owner. Crass as it had sounded, Selma made no apologies when she said women were props to Zander. At least until he'd met Molly. Of course, Molly really didn't believe that part of it.

She poured herself another glass of water and replaced the bottle on the ledge, label facing away. If she opened his cabinets, she'd probably find a good stock in antacids too. The man was a champion, driven to perfection—not only by his team, his sponsor, his owner—but by his own merit. He hated to lose. She'd seen that evidence by his reaction when luck didn't go his way. She wondered just what Zander had in his life, besides racing? Maybe an odd day at camp, visiting kids?

If she were in that position, she'd need a hell of a lot more than sleeping pills to keep her sane.

She flipped the kitchen light off and walked to the bedroom door. Zander was indeed still stretched out on top of the comforter, fast asleep. She leaned there and smiled. Why? Why did she have to feel, have to see this side of him, the broken boy within him that didn't seem to share himself with anyone else.

Extinguishing the dim bedroom lamp, she felt her way back to the bed. "Zander, c'mon, roll over." She nudged him.

He reached up and grabbed her, effectively wrapping her in his arms with one motion.

"Blanket?" she asked when he made no further moves. She tried to wriggle free, but he only pulled her tighter to him. His hard cock pressed against the crevice of her ass, making her wonder if he was sleeping at all.

She nudged backward and was rewarded by Zander's low groan against the back of her neck. Her body responded as if his hands had just touched every inch of her skin at once. She shuddered at the electricity that arced through her body when he lowered his teeth to her shoulder and grazed the flesh there.

"Cold?" he muttered.

"Nuh-uh." She pressed into him anyway, absorbing his body heat, knowing he could make her feel like she was about to combust.

"Hot?" he teased, laving his tongue over her collarbone and up the side of her neck. She shivered again.

"Gettin' there," she gasped, and arched back against him. She wanted him. She wouldn't be fulfilled until he was inside her.

"Hold on," he said, and rolled over. He was chuckling when he rolled back. "This is it, Mol. I'm out." He placed a square foil wrapper in her hands. "You want it now or in the morning?"

"Out?"

"Last one."

Heck, she'd never *had* to think about using more than three condoms in a night and now she was wondering how they were going to get by. "We'll get more tomorrow," she said. *If there is a tomorrow.*

"My thoughts exactly," he muttered. The bed shifted as he rolled over and straddled her hips. His cock pressed into the soft flesh of her stomach. His chest rubbed against the already aching peaks of her breast, the light pressure of his skin against her merely a teasing. She wanted more.

She opened her mouth to tell him so, but he covered her lips with his. His tongue stroked hers, fogging all her other senses.

How'd he get to her so quickly? Everything melted but this man, whose mouth grazed her lips with shivering sensitivity, then consumed her with his hungry demands. She gasped, missing him immediately as his lips left hers and trailed over her cheek, pausing to press a gentle kiss to her lips, her nose, her chin, each gesture doing nothing to diminish her desire, but taking her need to a new level. No longer would she be satisfied to have him physically—she wanted to bond with him emotionally as well.

She whimpered at the pressure she felt in her chest, a feeling so pure it nearly brought tears to her eyes.

When he kissed her again, she held him there, her hands framing his face as she memorized the texture of his stubble against her skin. He moaned as she pulled his bottom lip between her teeth and suckled, then released it to delve deep into his mouth and stroke his tongue with the same teasing intensity that he had done to her.

His hands tangled in her hair. He shifted his weight, lowering his body over hers and nudging his cock against the juncture of her thighs. She tilted her hips, biting down on his lip when the tip of his shaft pressed hard against her swollen clit.

Had it even been an hour since they had found release? How could her body feel starved for his touch already?

"You're killing me." His words mirrored her thoughts. "Get this damn thing on before I say fuck it and take you the way I want you."

Skin on skin. Oh, God, to feel him inside her without any barriers separating them. "Don't tempt me," she warned even as she felt around for the condom she'd dropped beside her. But he did, Lord, he did, rubbing the length of his cock along her slit and moving back and forth over the spot that was so sensitive it nearly hurt to touch.

"Get it on."

"I can't—I can't see and I've never—" Yet she didn't hesitate to reach for his cock the moment he lifted it away from her body. She stroked him, using her fingers to see him. Velvet over steel. She smiled, grateful he couldn't see her expression. She'd read that in romance novels yet never understood just how perfect the description was. She loved the feel of it in her hand, the slight raise of the veins that ran along the length, the way Zander jerked as she smoothed her finger along the slit. Fluid pooled there. She rubbed it in, smiling at his intake of breath as she squeezed his length and thrust him through her fist.

Her pussy clenched as she let him fuck her hand. Sex with Zander seemed so much more intimate than any of her previous encounters. She reveled in the way he reacted to her touch, even the simple pressure or friction against his cock, the way he sucked in his breath when she cupped his balls. How he continued to hold himself up that way while she touched and caressed him, she had no clue. Either he had amazing strength or an insane willpower.

"Condom. Now," he ordered, his voice strained. She stroked his cock once more, reluctant to let go of him. Her body ached for his touch, yes, but she was really enjoying the chance to pleasure him with her hands—and she'd add her mouth if he'd let her.

"Here." She thrust the packet against his chest. "I can't."

Without a word, he sat up. She heard the foil rip. What she wouldn't give to watch him. There were so many things about Zander she wanted to see, wanted to know. But those were forgotten when his hands encircled her ankles and his fingers tickled the inside her of legs. He worked his way up, nudging her thighs apart as he lightly massaged the flesh there. Her blood pounded in her ears. She practically shook in anticipation, loving every second of attention Zander gave her, but all too eager to sate her need.

Lord, she wanted him. At this point, she was almost as hungry to feel him lying in her arms as she was to have him inside her.

When his lips grazed her hip, in that sensitive spot at the crease of her thigh, she nearly came off the bed. "Stop it!" she hissed, trying to catch her breath. He would be the death of her yet. "That tickled."

"Did it now?" he teased, running his fingers over the place his mouth had just branded. "Does this tickle?" His breath grazed her belly first, raising goose bumps. Then his hot tongue hit her skin. It traced a line straight up the middle of her torso, dipping into her navel and then searing up between her breasts. As he worked his way up, he draped his body over hers.

His cock slipped between her thighs and pressed against her swollen clit. She arched up, needing him to be inside her, ending this torture.

"Christ, Molly," he whispered before covering her mouth with his. The slow motion of his hips against hers was maddening.

Finally, unable to take it any more, she reached between them and wrapped her hand around him. His heartbeat thudded against her chest. His body stiffened at her touch, a groan ripping from his throat as he thrust his tongue against hers.

She stroked him best she could, rubbing the head of his cock against her clit and then pressing it between the lips of her pussy the same way she used her vibrator at home. But this was so much more erotic. Her breathing was erratic, nearly a conscious effort. Despite doing the teasing herself, she murmured Zander's name as if pleading with him to make her come.

Finally, he thrust, breaching the swollen entrance. Her body bucked, her hips arching to pull him in. She whimpered as her muscles spasmed around him. God, he felt so good inside her, so thick, so full. The sweet friction of him as he moved, pulling out only to slide back in again had her crying out and clenching the bedding.

"Touch yourself," he whispered close to her ear. "That was hot."

Zander lifted his weight enough so she could slide her hand between their bodies and touch the place where he became part of her.

If only he could watch, God, that would be fucking incredible. He loved women who were confident enough to make themselves come. The fantasy of imagining Molly lying naked on his bed, legs spread, fingers buried inside her cunt had him damn near unable to control his own orgasm. Even now, her fingers brushed his cock and ball sack as she dipped her fingers into her pussy along side his cock and rubbed the moisture all over her clit. Fuck, that was hot.

He nuzzled her shoulder, hoping to distract himself until he could feel her orgasm building. He licked the hollow at the base of her neck, tasting the saltiness of sweat on her skin. She shuddered, making him want to nibble there again. How would she feel if he branded her the way he wanted to, the way his body—his soul—told him he should.

Her pace increased. He thrust harder, faster, to keep up with the motion of her hand against her clit. His muscles burned, his body so tight with need he thought he'd died from the pleasure-pain of waiting for her. She met each stroke with the rocking motion of her hips, driving him as deep inside her as he could go.

Making love to Molly was more than easing a physical need. She'd gotten under his skin and now his deepest desire was to touch her in ways she'd never been touched, love her like he had no other woman— the way no other man had ever had her.

Blind lust stole him then. She was his. He filled her with his cock over and over, claiming her, taking her, pushing both of them higher. He heard it in her cries, her gasps, felt it in the heartbeat that didn't seem to belong to either of them, but theirs together. He couldn't have stopped if he wanted to. He pushed harder, faster, punishing her to find his own climax, but knowing she was taking everything he gave her and loving it.

God, this woman was his. Until the day he died, he'd believe nothing less.

"Zander!" she screamed, his name trailing off into a wail accented by her gasps for breath. Her body convulsed under his. Her pussy clenched his cock as she came, pushing him past boundaries he never knew existed. When he came, he roared out before burying his face in her neck, inhaling her sweet scent and feeling her erratic heartbeat against his cheek.

He gave himself to her.

Unfuckingbelievable. He could barely breathe. Muscles all over his body ached. He still felt lightheaded from the lack of oxygen and rush of blood. He knew she had to feel the same way—worse with his weight on her. Reluctantly he rolled to the side, still keeping her body pressed against his.

He was so in trouble here. The kind of trouble that made him want to wrap her up and hide her away from the world—the media. The kind of trouble that made him question his desire to race—what would life be like with a woman like Molly, a normal day job, a dog, a few acres. He never questioned the sacrifices he'd made to race until now. Now they felt like a giant hole in his chest.

Carefully, he rolled away from her, then tugged the covers up over her. She didn't move, didn't speak. He prayed there was a reason for it—a reason far away from the thoughts that occupied his heavy heart.

Zander made his standard rounds, double checking the lock on the door and knobs on the gas stovetop. He got a drink, knowing it was futile to try to quench the thirst in him. It was just something he couldn't have. He'd lived with that feeling his entire life, so this shouldn't be any different. It just meant he'd have to concentrate a little harder on racing, focus a little more on the track.

Maybe in the off season he could look her up—far away from the ever present media hounds—and he could let her know how special she was to him for this weekend.

He sighed, then rubbed his hands through his hair. Never had sex been so good, yet life felt like it'd just issued a swift kick in the balls.

Chapter Nine

"I can't believe you're out," Molly said, lifting an eyebrow at the picture Zander made, standing nude in the doorway.

"Out of what?" He leisurely rubbed the towel over his hair. The rest of his skin glowed from the moisture of the shower. *Dayum,* he was fine.

"Condoms."

He grinned, his smile a little crooked. God. He hadn't bothered to shave, the stubble lining his cheeks a little darker this morning. She couldn't help licking her lips when he rubbed the towel across his chest and down over his hips. There wasn't a piece of flesh on him that wasn't prime. Hell, if he was ever to quit racing, he could model for a living. Though on second thought, no. Zander would never have the patience for that.

"We'll get some later." His eyes flitted over her body. She'd never regretted being dressed before. She could imagine him walking up to her, pulling her from where she sat at the side of the bed and pressing the full length of his body against hers. Both of them were still warm from the shower. God, she was getting turned on just imagining it.

She blinked a few times to erase that thought, only to look back up to see Zander standing in front of his closet. That vision left her breathless. The view from the back was as good as the one from the front. "Promise?" she barely squeaked out.

He caught her eye in the mirrored closet door. His wink had her squirming against the seam of her jeans. Damn that man.

Molly picked up her abandoned hairbrush and swung her hair around to brush the back—a chore she had been doing until he'd walked up to the doorway. She'd never get anything done with him parading around like that, teasing her. Zander Torris. Glancing around the room, the evidence she was indeed sitting on the bed of the NASCAR champ had her still savoring a sense of awe. Yet the man she knew last night was simply Zander, a man who hid so much of his real self from the world.

"You didn't promise." She hoped to keep the topic light. Her stomach did a flip-flop when he pulled on a sponsor shirt and adjusted the collar. She would lose him soon—lose him to the persona he hid behind.

"Maybe." Thank God the playful crinkles at the corner of his eyes were still present.

"Maybe?" She pouted, a little more dramatically than she normally would have. Desperate times call for desperate measures. "That's not very nice."

He shrugged on a pair of jeans and tucked his shirt in. "Yeah, but you still—" He stopped, swallowed, and then turned back around.

It was official—her heart came to a complete standstill. She knew what he was about to say, in fact, if he would have said it, she probably wouldn't have thought anything of it. But because he stopped...no. She was just reading way too much into it. He didn't say it because he didn't want the "L" word even cropping up between them. He didn't want to give her false hope.

"Yes, Zander," she said after swallowing a few times. She hoped her voice didn't give away the hollow feeling in her chest. "I still like you."

       🏁   🏁   🏁

"So." Molly eyed Zander over her glass of orange juice. He'd been much too quiet since his near-slip and it was driving her nuts to think this was going the way of a casual one-night stand—worse than that, one he regretted. "Are you going to lock me in here?"

Zander lifted an eyebrow—clearly his catchall gesture—but never stopped smearing grape jelly on his toast. "It'll make my day easier."

Molly nearly pounced on him, but then realized he finished his statement with a wide grin. Thank God. Still, he hadn't said no. "You wouldn't."

"No, I wouldn't."

"Not sure I should trust you," she leveled.

He licked the knife and laid it on the counter that doubled as bar. "Hmrph."

"So you'll let me tag along with you today?"

The look he gave her reminded her of dark clouds. Impending storms.

"I take that as a no."

"I've got some stuff this morning—couple of photo shots, an interview, meeting with sponsor reps and their families. I do those alone. You can hang around the garage or talk Selma into taking you shopping or something. I'll meet up with you right after lunch, okay?"

It's not like he gave her a choice, but honestly, did she expect him to drop everything to cater to her this weekend? "Sure, that works. I'd love to see more of the garage and maybe even meet some of the other drivers. Do you think it'd be uncool if I asked for autographs for my dad?"

His smile was the perfect one he saved for the camera. "I'm sure it'd be okay, if anyone's around. You've got to remember everyone has these tight schedules to keep. We don't have lots of time for socializing."

Yeah, she knew what he was trying to say. "Cool," she answered, smiling and then downing the rest of her juice.

The Zander she'd woken up beside had nearly completely faded into the Zander Torris everyone knew. His eyes were dark and shared nothing. He was intense, focused and cold as ice—well, almost.

"Give me a minute. I'll call Selma. She'll bring you a Kniola Automotive T-shirt to wear."

"Yeah?" she tried to sound excited, if only to make up for the lack of enthusiasm in his voice. She needed to make him quit purging his emotions like that, tucking them away or whatever he did.

"I'll see you later. I'm late." Zander dropped a kiss to her forehead and ducked out of the motorcoach.

*   *   *

"Zander," Steve hissed under his breath.

Zander started, glancing up into the curious eyes of his sponsor representatives. "I'm sorry, did I miss something? I was thinking about those milliseconds that kept us off the pole yesterday."

Thankfully, the gentlemen he was having a late breakfast with laughed appreciably. "That's what we like about you, Zander," Jack, the head honcho of Kniola Automotive said. "You're all business."

That earned Zander a kick under the table from Steve.

He just smiled and picked up his glass of water. Nothing, he realized, least of all water, was going to get Molly out of his head. When he'd walked out, he'd been close to saying something to wipe the smile off her face. Closer than he'd even gotten to the wall in turn four, which was dangerous territory. What he'd seen reflected back from her face had been far more than a casual, "see you later". If he didn't do something now, he was going to break her heart. And he wasn't going to get out of this unscathed either.

Another kick to the ankle pulled his attention back to the casual conversation. The business talk was over—and that was actually just the motions. How they wanted him to say their name during interviews and was he interested in doing another TV commercial? The real business talk took place behind corporate walls and, thank God, involved his team owner and the men who handled the money. Zander was happy to drive.

"What's with you?" Steve asked after they'd stood up, shook hands and said their good-byes. "They're worried about this distraction."

"I'm not distracted."

"Uh-huh. Her name Molly?"

"Fuck off, Steve. You know I don't get bent out of shape over women."

"Damn, Selma was right. This one *has* gotten to you."

His crew chief wisely remained out of slugging distance. "She's a sweet girl. And no, she's not like the chicks that hang out at the track, you know damn well the ones I've hooked up with were in it for the same reason I was. I don't think it's like that with Molly."

"I knew it. Can't believe I agree with Selma on this one, though. She's never gonna let me live it down."

Zander shook his head. He hated talking about his private life, but if he was going to do it, Steve was the one he could trust not to share it with anyone, including Selma if he asked him not to. And he wouldn't feed him any bullshit. Steve said what was on his mind.

"Forget about it, okay. I had a moment of chivalry and was overly concerned with her getting her heart broken."

"Keep it up and we'll never get your helmet on you."

Zander sighed. It wasn't about ego, at all. He hadn't tried to win her heart. Okay, maybe he had put a little more effort into wooing her for the dinner a couple of days ago than he would most women, but one act of kindness didn't make him worthy of falling in love.

Yet he'd managed to? Zander lifted his hand to his chest and pressed, hoping to alleviate the tightness there. Damn it, this wasn't supposed to happen.

"Indigestion?" Steve asked, his eyebrow arched a little too accusatorily for Zander.

He chose to ignore it. It'd be better if he just ignored the whole thing and let it go away. "Must be. Where to next?"

Zander strained to catch a glimpse of Molly as he rode through the garage area on the back of his golf cart after dropping Steve off. He couldn't stop, though. He was scheduled to sign autographs and meet fans for two hours at his merchandise trailer. Normally he didn't mind—it was always busy and the time went fast.

Today it was the last thing he wanted to do.

"Hey guys."

"Z, ready to do this?"

His gas man and jack man, the biggest guys on his over-the-wall team, accompanied him through the throng of people. He hated needing the escort, but the press of excited fans could get dangerous. The fans were what made the sport. They were loyal—damn loyal to the sponsors and their car number. Seems like everyone in the crowd wore a driver shirt or hat. It was always a thrill to see his car on someone's chest, but the followings had gotten so big, he couldn't stop and thank the individual people any more.

"Keep pushing."

Zander felt the hands grabbing at him as he threaded his way through the crowd already gathered at his trailer. Driver signings were well advertised and well attended. Shame he couldn't get to all these people in his two-hour increment.

Despite his worries, his two hours went quickly. As he signed one last ball cap for a young girl, he spotted Molly and Selma making their way down merchandise alley. "Hey," he called to Shane, his gas man. "Go tell them to wait."

Zander said a few words in parting to the crowd, the rehearsed speech he gave every week, which thanked them for their loyalty and that he would do his best to win this week's race just for them. But his eyes drifted beyond the people standing in front of him and locked on Molly.

His heart did flip-flops watching her shield her eyes and grin up at Shane. Then Selma nudged her and she looked right at him.

He stumbled through the end of his talk, forcing his eyes back to the crowd and meeting the gaze of as many fans as he could.

As the crowd moved on, he sat in the corner of the narrow display trailer and waited. Too bad waiting made him think, and right now that was a bad thing. He'd been jealous of the coy smile she'd flashed at Shane, probably accompanied by some light sarcasm about being summoned to the trailer. Selma would have dished it on heavier, but Zander wasn't worried. Steve had more or less admitted Selma was determined to play matchmaker—so she wouldn't pass up a chance to flaunt Molly in front of him.

"Excuse me, Zander?" The young girl who rang up sales summoned him.

"Yeah?" He didn't want to get up and attract too much attention.

"Can you do one more autograph?"

Selma grabbed Molly's arm and stopped her. "Hold on."

"What?"

They stepped out of the middle of the busy thoroughfare. "Ten to one Zander will have me get them tickets or pit passes."

"Who?" Molly couldn't see what the heck Selma was talking about.

"Look, see the two pairs of jeans and the wheelchair? That's Zander and a father and son."

"Oh. *Oh*." She squinted to see a little better. "Little boy?"

"Yeah. Zander's a sucker for underprivileged kids."

"Like the camp." It made sense. It also made her react to him in ways she could explain. It would have been easy if she could peg him as an egotistical, self-serving asshole.

"Zander's a good man."

Molly knew where Selma was going. "Uh huh."

"He's very private, but loyal as the day is long. Loves kids. Loves racing, hates the attention. He'd race if it weren't televised. Would probably prefer it. But he does it."

"Uh huh," she repeated. She was only half listening to Selma anyway. Zander had crouched down beside the wheelchair, she could see half of his body as he leaned in and communicated with the boy. While it didn't surprise her—she'd long known most racers were big on children's charities and she had overheard Zander talking to the boy at the camp—she was not prepared for the way it made her breath catch, her pulse race, her heart threaten to explode from her chest. Who wouldn't fall for a man who took the time out to talk to a kid like that? One who singled out a troubled boy and challenged him to succeed. And who thought ahead enough to arrange for his date to have suitable clothes for a night out.

She was history, toast. It was over, she was smitten, and she hadn't even factored the amazing sex into it.

Damn shame it was Zander Torris, because there was about a snowflake's chance in hell that even an iota of her feelings would be returned.

"Yep, you've got it."

"Huh?" Molly blinked and turned to Selma who stood staring at her, one hand on her hip.

"You're in love with him."

"Am not."

"Are too. I can see it written on your face."

"I'm sure all Zander's weekend dates look like this."

Selma sighed. "You're terrible. But simply adorable. I can see why Zander's so head over heels for you."

"He is not," Molly insisted, digging in her heels as Selma tried to pull her toward where he stood with the boy and his father.

"Oh please. Trust me. Let's go. He'll be calling me any second."

True to what she said, when they rounded the side of the merchandise trailer, Zander closed his phone. "I was just going to call you."

"I saw you," she said to Zander, then turned. "Hi, I'm Selma. This is Molly. You are?" She held her hand out and shook each of their hands. Molly was amazed with this woman, so vivacious and friendly.

"They don't have tickets for tomorrow."

"Done. Zander, why don't you take Molly with you back to the coach, I'll catch up after I get some information from these two hunky men here." She whipped out her PDA and started taking down their names.

"I'll see you guys tomorrow, then, right?"

"'Bye, Zander. Thanks! I hope you win!" The boy had the biggest blue eyes that glittered like diamonds as he looked up at them.

"Thank you. I can't thank you enough. This means so much to him," the boy's father said, nearly choking on his words. Molly blinked back tears.

"Be here, that's thanks enough. Wave at me as I go by." Zander reached out and tweaked the hat of the little boy, then took Molly's elbow.

"That was sweet of you," she said after they'd walked several yards in silence. Of course, the two crew guys flanked them, allowing them virtually no privacy—if that sort of thing even existed at the racetrack.

"Nah, it's nothing. Poor little guy couldn't get up to the trailer to get anything signed. The crowds are mobs. I hate signings like I did today. Little people like that—the ones I want to see—get crushed."

"Still, getting them tickets, that's going an extra step." Her body hummed as Zander rested his hand at the small of her back to steer her through the maze of temporary trailers and buildings. They ducked under a roped off area. She couldn't get over how the fans followed, shouting Zander's name as they walked out of the tunnel that ran under the track. He probably would have given autographs, but it would have turned into another of the mob scenes he'd described.

"I've got to go to the garage and talk to Steve. Why don't you go on to the hauler and I'll meet you there in just a few minutes. I've got to change before my next sponsor meeting." His breath was hot against the side of her neck, his mouth inches from her. It made her lungs tighten, despite her attempts not to react to him.

"Um, sure."

Warm fingers lingered at her waist then slipped away. She shivered. Molly bet his mind was already on other stuff—his car, his schedule, his crew. The garage area was incredibly busy, as the Busch series pre-race ceremonies were in full swing. She wasn't as versed on that series, at least as far as names and sponsors and car numbers were concerned. She'd still like to watch, though—to feel the thunder as they came down for the green flag, the vibration in her chest as the horsepower filled the entire infield with at deafening decibels.

Maybe they'd let her crawl up on top of the hauler to watch the race. She'd done that once, back when she was a teenager. Stood on top of a toolbox on an open trailer and watched the cars go around and around. That had been a thrill on the little three-eighths mile track. She'd gone home with dust coating her face and hair, her hands black with grease from helping load the car when it was done. She'd been the unofficial spotter on a Saturday night feature for one of her father's friends who raced locally and had been hooked on the sport every since.

Regardless of what happened with Zander, there was something about the pulse of auto racing that called to her, lured her in. She loved the excitement, and here, the grand scale of things. Sure, she could understand Zander's frustration with the media. Even now, flashbulbs popped behind the chain link fence as she cut between haulers until she got to the one housing Zander's equipment.

A luxury semi, not unlike his luxury motorcoach. She knocked hesitantly at the door. Nothing. Probably all in the garage, reviewing or practicing or whatever it was they did on Saturday afternoons. She tried the door, surprised to find it unlocked.

"Molly, right?"

She jerked her hand back from the door, and sputtered to explain what she was doing. "Z-Zander told me to, uh…wait here for him. He um, went to the garage."

"It's cool." He nudged his thick glasses back up his nose. "I'm Mike, suspension specialist. This is my office."

"How'd you know my name?" She stood her ground, at least until she realized he expected her to pull the door open and enter ahead of him. It wasn't that she didn't feel comfortable with him, it just seemed much too strange to be allowed in all these places without her credentials being checked and double checked—or having Zander there to vouch for her.

"We all know your name." His answer was complete, but frustrating. Probably intentionally cryptic.

"So you're in charge of setting up springs and shocks?"

"Not so much today. I do a lot of my research in tests and practice runs. We use that data and feedback from Zander and the crew to determine what combination we're going to put on the car for race day. I'm just going over what we've got."

Molly stood beside him as he passionately described the spring rubber and its affect on the lean of the car. She learned about camber, and how to adjust it, and then Mike launched into a description of how track bar or wedge adjustments helped different ailments. Like she was going to remember that.

Half tuning him out, she admired the sterile precision of the hauler. It was really nothing more than a long hallway with counters and cabinets and hundreds of drawers on each side. Most of them opened like toolboxes and lined with foam. To protect everything while in transit, Mike explained.

It was state of the art. Hundreds of thousands of dollars invested in just this rig. Yet it was the heart of the racing operations when they were at the track. Complete engines, transmissions and rear axles were stored in there. In fact, she already knew there was an entire race car stored just above the ceiling, in case Zander had wrecked his primary car during practice or qualifying.

She let Mike talk, humored with the excitement he had for his job, and kept watching the entrance for Zander.

"Hey, check it out. This explains why Zander's left you waiting." Mike turned a monitor toward her and turned up the volume.

Zander was talking into a microphone, but refusing to look into the camera. He rattled off a speech about qualifying and how he hoped to improve his race finish by one position.

"So," asked the unseen interviewer. "What's the secret behind your good fortune this weekend?"

"The point chase is getting tight and—"

"Absolutely. Any truth to the rumor that you've finally settled down from your trademark bachelor days?"

"I'm still a bachelor if that's what you mean."

Molly could barely stand to watch, her fists clenched for Zander as the man pried into a personal life he had no business asking about. She was pissed for him!

"Really? A source has hinted the woman you were seen with earlier this week at a benefit dinner is sporting a ring. And isn't she here this weekend to cheer you on?"

Mike dropped several tools, which clanged off the diamond plate counter top. Then went into a coughing fit.

Molly ignored him, but stepped closer to the monitor to study Zander's reaction to the suggestion they were engaged. She didn't need to look at her hands. She did wear a ring, a square cut aquamarine—on her middle finger of her left hand. It had been her mother's.

"It wasn't my idea she come this weekend, or any weekend. I don't know where you all get your information, but if she's wearing a ring, you can be quite sure I didn't give it to her." He took a deep breath, and before the interviewer could say another word, turned and walked off. The camera stayed on his back as he departed. Zander's ears were red, his hands, like hers, clenched into fists.

"I'm outta here," Mike said. The way his eyes darted toward the door made her nervous. "He's not going to be happy when he gets here."

"Sure, leave me with him," Molly muttered as Mike grabbed sunglasses and practically ran out the door. "Chicken," she called after him, but only when he was too far away to hear.

"Not my idea," she repeated Zander's words as she paced the length of the truck. "You can be sure I didn't give it to her." *No, but you were more than happy to use me as arm candy the other night.* Her temper built the more she thought about it. What happened to let's toy with the media and get them to talk? What happened with Zander the man who hid his total private life behind the lies he fed to the press? He laid it all on the line there, didn't he? At her expense. Nice.

"Thanks a lot!" she said as she launched at him the moment she saw him and jabbed her fingers into his chest. "You make me sound like some crazed fan following you around the damn track. Don't worry, Zander, I got the message loud and clear this morning that there wasn't anything between us after this weekend, you didn't have to broadcast it for the entire world to hear just now."

"What are you talking about?" There was actually a bit of laughter in his voice, but the smile died when he looked at her. Oh yeah, she was steaming. Big time.

"I don't know you. A few nights ago I was nothing more than your arm candy. You even dressed me like I was some Barbie doll. I should have known you'd never invite me here, and I was right. You're all about what Zander wants, when Zander wants it. But since I was here, I decided to enjoy my stay, and please, don't tell me you didn't enjoy my stay, too. Nice slap in the face on TV. Thanks."

"Molly, I—"

"Shut up and listen to me. I know what you're doing with this pseudo persona you put on when the cameras are rolling. But it's making the rest of us insane—hell, I don't know how your crew stands you because I've been here less than twenty-four hours and I'm ready to kill you. It's like the public Zander has to denounce anything and everything personal to him. You're not a robot, Zander. The media is digging because they know about your game—you're the one who started it and set the rules. I'm fair game."

"I was trying to—"

"Protect me? From who? You, or the men and women out there whose job is to get the latest scoop on the NASCAR gigolo?"

"Molly, dammit." He sighed and pushed his hand through his hair.

Her chest rose and fell as she regarded him. His jaw was set, his mouth drawn into a tight line. His eyes were narrowed, hiding any emotion. Just like he did on TV.

"You know what? My being here is a mistake." She willed herself not to cry, her voice not to let her down. "I wish I hadn't have come. I wish I hadn't have met the Zander who took time out for a little confused boy back at the camp, for a man who took a moment for a boy in a wheelchair and then went an extra step so he could see the race. For the man who made love to me last night. Great as it was, Zander Torris, I wish I had never met you."

Chapter Ten

Zander grabbed Molly, slid his hand behind her head and tilted that lovely mouth up so he could devour her whole. His intention was to shut her up, to make her stop saying things he didn't want to hear out loud.

The pain in her eyes belied her words. She didn't hate him at all. He'd hurt her, he knew that, and damn, it hurt him just to see evidence of it. He wasn't liking himself very much at the moment.

She struggled to free herself from his grasp, shoving and pummeling his chest even as she parted her lips to let him plunder her mouth. She moaned against the strokes of his tongue. He curled his fingers in her hair, holding her against him, loving every bit of fire that raged through her.

It wasn't until her fist stopped pounding and turned to gripping his shirt that he released her mouth. He backed up slowly, running his finger through her hair and studying her face. She was confused, probably as much as he was.

Damn Selma and her meddling. But it wasn't all her fault. Molly had come, but Zander had insisted she stay with him, had really started it all by inviting Miss Molly, the camp nurse, to dinner.

That seemed like weeks ago, not merely days. Yet the woman he looked at now still had an innocent surprise on her face, a look of awe that reminded him of when he bought her the expensive outfit. The image was seared into his mind and would likely haunt him for the rest of his days.

"Excuse me." She reached up to touch her lips. The very gesture made his mouth water, despite the iciness in her tone. "But I'm not quite fluent in speaking in tongues. What was it you were saying?"

He laughed at her. Of course, all that seemed to do was piss her off more, but he couldn't help it. She was a spitfire, so passionate. He'd love to see that aggression played out in the bedroom. But considering they weren't in the bedroom…

"C'mere, I'll try to go slower this time."

"You are not going to gloss over such a public betrayal like that by trying to kiss me senseless."

"I'm not trying to kiss you senseless."

"You're trying to change the subject."

"It's a much better subject."

"Zander," she growled through gritted teeth. Did the woman have any idea that the more she pushed, the hotter he got? Clearly not.

He'd just have to push back. "You have any idea how much I like to hear you say my name that way?" He took a step closer, forcing her to back up against the counter or be pressed against his body.

Now, just to get her naked and sitting on the edge. He licked his lips in anticipation.

"You're looking at me like I'm prime rib and you're a hungry wildcat."

"I'm hungry all right. And you are prime."

"Your lines are getting cornier and cornier. Can't we have a decent, serious conversation here?"

"Later," he said, leaning forward and placing his hands on the counter, successfully pinning her in place. He nuzzled her neck, chuckling as she twisted her head away. There was nowhere for her to go. Even when Molly was in a fighting mood, she was much more fun to deal with than those asinine media people.

"Zander, please. You can't just expect me to pretend I didn't hear what you said."

"Oh, but I do," he muttered, yet braced for her to slug him. She didn't, just sighed dramatically. Which was enough to sober him up—a little. "Okay." He gave her a little space, but made sure he stayed between her and the door. "Why do I have to explain to you my feelings about those stupid reporters? I thought—"

"First night, I was arm candy. Cool, fine, I can live with that. I get here and you're hiding me away like I'm some kind of leper or something. Are you embarrassed of me?"

He tried to kiss her, to prove to her that he was anything but. She shook him off. "Of course I'm not. I was trying to protect you."

"This is beginning to sound like a broken record. I don't need protection. Except perhaps from you. So far you've made me feel rather unwelcome, but then of course, you spirited me away to your coach so you could have a little fun, then you locked me in there, and heaven forbid I walk around without an escort." She blew upward, causing her hair to lift off her forehead before falling back into her eyes.

He reached up to push it out of the way, but she batted his hand down. He chuckled at her.

"Don't you say a word, Torris. Not a word."

Of course he had to. "You've told me this already. Now why can't we take advantage of the fact that we've got this place to ourselves?"

"Damn you." She dropped her fists onto his chest and laughed. "You are the most despicable man I've ever met. I don't want to hear things like you had to just say on TV. Even though I know you think you're protecting me, I hate it. You don't know how much I want to hate you right now for not letting me stay mad at you."

"I think you were telling me rather well. And since it's not something I want to hear, I think the conversation should—" he kissed her nose, "—be over." He brushed his lips over hers, then let go of the counter to cradle her face in his hands. "You are so damn beautiful. I've thought about you all day. And I promise I won't be so…protective of you, even though hiding you away and not sharing you with any one else has its merit."

Her eyes widened, her lips parted, which was all the invitation he needed. He swore she pulled him to her, their mouths dueling for the lead while their bodies burned at each point of contact.

He'd never lusted after a woman this badly—he was rock hard and aching for her. And he did speak the truth, she'd haunted him no matter what he did. While it pissed him off then that he couldn't get her out of his mind, right now she consumed him to the point of madness. He had to have her.

He was rough, maybe too rough. Her scent filled his nostrils, her barely perceptible moans and whimpers teasing his ears. He wanted to crush her against him until neither of them could tell where he ended and she began. He wanted, no needed, to possess her.

"Zander," she breathed his name between kisses. His body reacted the same way his car did when he jammed the gas pedal to the floorboards. No way was he stopping until the race was over. And he had every intention of winning.

Willing himself to be gentle, he lifted her to the counter and positioned himself between her spread legs. Imagining her without those bothersome jeans was damn near his undoing. He wanted to touch her. Her skin was magical—soft, hot, delicious. Like a drug. He never thought he'd find anything as addicting as speed, but Molly was in contention for that trophy. No matter how many times he kissed her, he was all the more hungry for her lips. The more he touched her, the more he needed to.

With a growl, he tugged her shirt up and closed his hands over her breasts. She sighed and leaned back, thrusting the tight peaks into his palms. He squeezed them, then rolled her nipples between his thumb and forefingers until she whimpered for him to stop. He replaced his fingers with his mouth, taking a moment to tease the flesh along the lace that covered her pretty breasts before unsnapping the front clasp and taking her breasts full into his hands.

"Damn. Just a minute." He darted to the door and flipped the lock. No way did he want company and he wasn't sure he'd have remembered the lock once her jeans came down.

"Your turn." Molly reached for his shirt when he returned.

Silently thanking every power-that-ever-was, he lifted his hands and let her pull his shirt loose from his jeans.

He closed his eyes and reveled in the exploring touch of her fingers across his bare stomach. His nipples tightened—who knew he'd experience such awareness from the mere act of her brushing her thumb over them.

His gut tightened as her eyelids fluttered closed and her lips parted. His cock was painfully hard, but there was something else going on, something he didn't care to analyze, but it scared him to death. He breathed her in, relishing the velvety texture of her firm breasts. Her heartbeat thudded against his hands. Had he ever noticed a woman's heartbeat before?

He swallowed and fought to control the emotion that swept over him. This wasn't supposed to happen. This was supposed to be about quenching a physical need. But there was no lying to himself. She'd gotten to him. Big time.

Shoving such thoughts out of the way, he focused on her bare skin. With slow strokes, he ran the back of his hands over her shoulders and down her arms. She shuddered beneath his touch, making his cock throb painfully.

He nearly laughed with relief when she grabbed his hands and placed them over her breasts. He kneaded her flesh, cupping the weight and lowering his mouth to the rosy peaks that stood out and begged for tasting. She whimpered and threaded her fingers through his hair and held him there.

Unable to see but driven with determination, he fumbled with the snap on her jeans until the material parted and he could tease the soft flesh of her stomach beneath.

"No fair," she said as she slid off the counter. "I can't reach you."

"You don't need to." Yet he understood her frustration. At the current angle, he wasn't going to get his hand where he wanted it either.

"How do you normally seduce your women in here?" she asked, a tell-tale twinkle in her eye.

"Mike normally doesn't allow women in here. Feel privileged." He advanced on her. She backed up, never breaking eye contact. Out of the corner of his eye, he saw her feel around until she snagged a makeshift weapon. Though he wasn't sure what she had in mind for the air driven impact wrench she held.

"Privileged? You're taking advantage of me in a car hauler."

He laughed at the mock southern accent she used. "I could say that you lured me in here to seduce me...you know, for my money and all."

She snorted and aimed the gun at him. When she pulled the trigger, the socket whirled noisily. He'd never been afraid of the tool his crew used to loosen the lug nuts on the wheels of his car before, but in her hand, pointed at his midsection, he couldn't help but be nervous.

"I'd rather you didn't do that," he said, putting one hand over his throbbing cock, which was more turned on than worried over a woman with a power tool. "My nuts don't need tightening, thanks."

Laughing, Molly lunged forward, holding the air ratchet a little lower than he was comfortable with.

"That isn't the kind of screwing I had in mind..." There was simply not enough room in this narrow corridor. He backed into a row of drawers, then leapt forward, dropping his shoulder and turning to keep all ultra-sensitive parts away from spinning metal. Not that he thought she'd hurt him, not at all. This was a game, and he had an idea.

Zander had the strength advantage and quickly had her arm pinned to her side. She hit the trigger. He yelped, more to scare her than due to the brush of a rapidly spinning socket against his forearm. It did the trick, for she froze. He took advantage—and the impact wrench.

"My turn." he grinned evilly. "Though I think I need a slightly smaller socket for the tips of your breast, what do you think, three-eights or a quarter inch?" He revved the air gun near her chest to emphasis.

"Oh, no you don't." He laughed as she tried escaping. He backed her into the corner, pressing kiss down her neck as he toyed with the trigger. He was careful not to get close enough to her delicate flesh. Spinning like it did, the socket could get hot and if there were any rough edges, it would act like a bit and dig in.

"Zander!" she yelped as he slid his hand down the back of her loosened jeans and cupped her ass.

"Yes, dear?" he asked, reluctantly slipping his hand back up, smoothing over the contour of her lower back and groove of her spine. The woman was enchanting. Everything about her made him nuts. Unable to think. Okay, think about anything *but* sex.

"This was supposed to be quick."

"It was?"

Her teasing demeanor burned his gut. When was the last time he'd joked during sex? Ever? Is this what couples did?

"Put that...that...tool thing away and hurry up."

"This?" He nudged the top of it along her waist, over her hipbone and across the juncture of her thighs. He held the socket part well out of the way so that if he hit the trigger, all she'd feel was the vibration of the ratchet. In fact...

"Zander!" she squealed, flattening herself against the metal cabinets behind her. "What was that?"

His free hand snaked around until he could grab a belt loop and hold her steady. Then he nudged the top of the air wrench just below her zipper and squeezed the trigger gently. The vibration was subtle, but judging from her gasp, she felt it against her clit as he intended.

"Like that?"

"What are you doing?"

"Giving you a tune-up?" he countered before releasing the trigger and pulling her body against his. Damn, this woman made him insane. She was so receptive, so sensual, yet managed to strike a chord within him with her tousled innocence. Her cheeks were flushed, her eyes bright, curious. He read lust there, but there was something more to her, something that made it possible to laugh during sex.

"The counter is going to be cold," he warned her.

"Mmmm." She sighed against his lips, then pressed her tongue inside. "What exactly does a tune-up require?"

He tilted his head for better access to her mouth and swiped the length of her tongue with his, then suckled hers until her weight sagged against him. When he pulled away, he answered, "Checking fluids. So far so good."

Sliding his free hand around her waist he said. "Body feels solid."

She giggled. He watched her face as her emotions reflected in her widening eyes and quivering lips. It was fun. And funny. And sexy as hell.

"What are you doing now?"

His fingers smoothed upward until reaching the swell of her breasts, then he circled each of them, tighter and tighter circles until he tugged at one, then the other breast. Her breathing came harder, her heart pounded beneath soft skin. "Headlights. Yeah. Just, um, making sure they're...working."

"Working?"

They bounced against his hand as she full out laughed.

"Yeah," he said, defending himself. "Work with me here."

"Go on." Her stomach pulsated beneath his fingers as she continued to giggle at his antics.

"Let me guess," she teased when he dipped a finger into her navel. "Checking the oil?"

"Um, I was thinking that of more like an ignition switch."

"Interesting," she said.

He lowered the air impact wrench to their feet and swept her shirt up so he could see where his fingers were exploring. Kissing the skin around her navel, he traced the line of her jeans with his tongue, dipping into the divot before teasing lower.

"I can't possibly do a proper diagnostic with these in the way." He tugged at her jeans. The scent of her body in this small space was enough to make his mouth water.

"Well, I couldn't leave here without the full tune-up you promised me."

He growled and knelt before her. With a fist full of denim in each hand, he tugged. The way she wriggled her hips as the material peeled off those luscious curves of her hips made him blind to everything but her. He wanted to lean forward and bury his face in her cunt, to lap at her folds and tease that ripe bud until they brought the walls of the hauler down around them.

Knowing that sometimes the fastest car didn't win the race, he forced himself to exercise patience. He nudged the material down around her ankles, then encircled her calves with his hands and tested her flesh, working his way up one leg and down the other.

It was comforting to hear her breathing increase as he neared the downy curls at the top of her thighs, the sharp, almost inaudible gasp as his thumb grazed lightly over her there.

Smiling despite his driving need to forget their little game and bury himself to the hilt inside her, he ran a finger along her folds and withdrew it, the glistening moisture of her arousal coating his hand. He stood up to face her. "You've got a leak." His voice betrayed his teasing tone. It sounded foreign to him, so low and husky.

"I do?"

"Yep." He looked her in the eye, then licked the juices off. "It's a serious problem we need to correct right away. And there's only one solution for that."

"Well?" she demanded, reaching for the button of his jeans and fumbling to get it open. By the time she had the zipper down, he had two fingers inside her, stroking the walls of her tight pussy.

"This leak definitely needs to be plugged. Can you imagine if I just let it go?"

She whimpered and rubbed his cock through his jeans and briefs. He released her, only to lower his pants out of the way and release his cock to her eager hands. He had to grip the counter behind Molly for balance as she stroked his length, then smoothed his fluid over the top.

"Zander?" she asked. "Get over here and fix it."

"My pleasure." He cupped her face with his hands and took her mouth in a kiss that ended all teasing. She wrapped her arms around his neck, making him curse the layers of their shirts that prevented him from feeling the taut points of her breasts against his chest. He sat her up on the counter, smiling against her lips at the soft moan that escaped her. The counter was cold, but he'd get her heated up so quickly she wouldn't even notice.

With his help, she kicked one leg free of the confining jeans and then locked her ankles behind his back. The counter was the perfect height. After digging the foil packet out of his pants and donning the condom, he guided the head of his cock against her wet center, sighing at the pleasure of the intimate contact.

When her fingernails dug into his shoulder, he pushed inside her.

She did the rest, using the pressure on his back to set the blistering pace. Her cunt was so hot, so wet as she enveloped him—all of him. He closed his eyes to keep from staring at how uninhibited she was, her lips parted, her cheeks flushed, her eyelashes resting against her cheeks. Even as the passion built inside him, harder and stronger, his chest tightened, unable to erase the image of her and simply take his own pleasure.

She came first. He caught her mouth to muffle her cries as she shuddered against him. Nails dug into his back, spurring him to increase his pace until he, too, let the pleasure take him over the edge. Groaning, he buried his face against her neck until the sensations subsided.

"So," Molly asked, still a little breathless. "Do you think you fixed the leak?"

He laughed, still inside her. The motion sent aftershocks throughout her body, making her shiver in his arms. "If that didn't do it, nothing will."

"And here I just thought you were the driver, not the mechanic."

"I've got a lot of talents," he said, grazing her forehead with his lips.

Molly damn near had to blink back tears. Why couldn't Zander be like this all the time—playful, teasing, willing to open up and love? Maybe he didn't realize he shut himself off the way he did. She hoped what she'd said earlier had sunk in.

"Add seducing women in the car hauler as another one," she teased as they righted their clothes. She smoothed her hair, but knew there was little she could do from looking like she'd just had a romp in the… Oh God, she'd just had sex with Zander Torris in his car hauler. What was she thinking? *That it was damn near the best sex of my life.*

She smiled up at Zander, who returned the look, his eyes softening. It made her heart race. It gave her hope—hope she shouldn't look for, but dammit, how could she not get her heart involved? It was too late, had been too late, and each encounter like this was only making her fall more and more in love with a man she could never have.

"Did you mean what you said?" she asked, holding her breath while he studied her face, brows knit.

"What did I say?"

"That you promised not to be so protective."

"Um, yeah, I guess so. I just worry the media people are going to pounce on you. And I want to be the only one doing the pouncing."

"I can take care of myself," she warned, still holding the smile, but watching the light in his eyes disappear. He was hiding that personal side again. "I won't talk to them. I won't talk to anyone you haven't already introduced me to. But I didn't come here to be a caged bird. I really don't like how you treat me like a different person in public. Wait, I forgot, you won't take me in public."

"This isn't an amusement park. It's serious business."

"This," she spit out, waving her hand around the hauler with all its tools, parts and machinery. "This is business but you sure were intent on mixing pleasure with it, weren't you?"

He looked away.

That said enough.

"I'm going to go out and sit in the stands and watch the Busch race. Then I'll watch your practice. I'll do my best to forget there's a side to Zander Torris you refuse to acknowledge, a side I made the dumb mistake of falling in love with."

She twisted the lock, shoved open the door, barely registering the shocked face of Mike and two other guys wearing Kniola Automotive logos on their shirts.

She was past caring. Praying she remembered how to get back to Zander's motorcoach, she cut through the row of haulers and averted her face to the fans and media lined up along the chain link fence. She heard someone call her name, but ignored it.

"Molly!"

This time she recognized it as Selma. She turned back to find her friend racing toward her. "Where have you been? Where's Zander? Josh's been looking all over for him."

"Check his hauler."

"Hauler?" Selma grabbed Molly's arm and turned her around. Molly cast a look at the fans gathering up close to the fence near where they stood.

"He was in there...talking to Mike."

Selma's eyes roved over her, but then she frowned. "Things not good?"

"Oh everything's wonderful. Zander's just great. Great." She reached up to swipe at a tear when the flashbulb went off in her face.

Chapter Eleven

"Let's get out of here." Selma grabbed Molly's elbow and led her away from the fans. "I take it you don't have a key to Zander's coach."

"Oh, of course not."

"Steve's talking to the tire changers in ours—impromptu meeting. Let's just go to the garage."

Molly looked down on herself and smoothed her shirt.

"Trust me, no one will notice. Most of 'em are out watching the race anyway." The Busch cars had taken the track. Soon it would be difficult to talk without shouting, at least up in the garage area.

"I came here to be a race fan, not be his one girl harem." Molly attempted a weak smile. "Screw him. Let me be your guest. Show me around."

"I can do that," Selma said with a wink and looped her arm through Molly's.

No way was she going to let Zander totally ruin this weekend. She couldn't—wouldn't—deal with his split personality and controlling nature. What had happened in the hauler had been as much her doing as Zander's, but a spicy sex life couldn't erase the fact that there was no hope for a relationship, this weekend, this lifetime. That was clear in the fact he'd been willing to tell her what he wanted to hear just to get her pants off.

"Stop thinking," Selma chided, nodding toward the garage. "Looks like lover boy has beat you here. The best revenge is acting like you don't care."

Molly's mouth went dry when she looked up and watched Zander run his hand over the fender before leaning beneath the hood to see whatever the guy next to him was talking about. He sure looked like he didn't care.

"Maybe we shouldn't go in there." Coward's way out, she knew, but she hadn't had time to think, to get her bearings, to plan how she was going to get out of here with at least part of her heart intact. Just looking at him made her react. She could barely tear her eyes from him to look at the car, the toolboxes, the other guys hard at work underneath the car. "They look busy."

Steve came around the corner, spotted them and then shook his head.

"See?" Molly said. "Very busy."

"That's not what he's saying. Trust me." Selma kept walking. "Why are you afraid of him?"

"I'm not!" she insisted, perhaps a little too loudly.

"Not what?" Steve asked.

"She's afraid to come in here and bother you guys."

Molly gritted her teeth and shot Selma a look she'd like to back up with a swift elbow to the ribs. Clearing her throat, she smiled, but sinking through the pavement sounded like a better idea. "I don't want to be in the way. You all look busy. Selma promised me a tour."

"I'll give you a tour," Zander spoke up, taking a step toward them.

"Oh no, I don't want to keep you from working."

"I'm sure the guys want me out of their hair so they can get this engine changed."

The guys behind him nodded in agreement. Steve made a sweeping motion with his hand. Even Selma nodded.

"Engine change? Doesn't that send you to the back of the field tomorrow?" How could he be smiling if he was facing such a set back? There was a huge difference between starting second and starting forty-third.

"I'd rather start dead last at Talladega then have an engine let go and finish there."

"True." She remembered the last race there were several drivers who intentionally dropped to the back of the draft to avoid the bumping and banging that could potentially cause "the big one", the wreck that happened all too often at these restrictor plate tracks and wiped out half the field.

"We need to talk," he said, leaning closer to her ear.

"What's that going to solve?" she challenged. She wanted to yell, but was careful to keep her voice out of earshot of his crew.

"Walk."

She had no choice, he gripped the back of her jeans and steered her out of the garage and in the opposite direction of pit lane. "You are not taking me back to your motorcoach." She stopped in her tracks.

"Well, I'd rather not bare my soul in public," he retorted. The lines of his face were deeper, harsher. A cold, stony stare replaced the fiery gaze he'd leveled at her earlier. It chilled her right to the bone. Or rather, right to the heart.

"That's the problem, Zander. What are you so afraid of?"

"I can't believe you're asking that." He started walking again.

She dug her heels in. The force of his stride damn near yanked her off her feet. "I don't get it. Why do you go out of your way to flaunt lies to the media? They only search you out because you perform like some damn circus monkey for them. They know it'll sell."

"You don't see the other drivers 'fessing up their life story."

"They don't have to. But they don't live a lie, either." She put her hands on her hips and narrowed her eyes, trying like hell to intimidate him.

He just rolled his eyes, shook his head and tugged. "I won't let them destroy my personal life."

She sensed there was something unsaid there, but for a split second, the raw pain that flitted across his face, twisting his features into a sad grimace, silenced her sarcastic comeback. *Ah-hah*, there is a reason.

"You don't *have* a personal life, Zander. There's no need to be dragging me off and locking me up somewhere in some mock attempt at protection. I'll tell the media just what you did. I'm nobody. Just a friend you made at the camp. In exchange for taking me to dinner, you got me a pass to the race. You can go on your merry way, I'll go back to my life."

"Molly, I—"

"You've said enough." She swallowed, then lifted her chin higher and looked him full in the face. It was impossible not to feel pain, a choking ache that started in her chest and radiated outward. Her stomach knotted, her head pounded and tears lingered just beneath the surface, ready to pour down her cheeks. But not right now, that was for later, when she was alone. She refused to let him see how much power he had over her. She'd been a fool to think she, a nurse practitioner from Nowhere, Ohio, could catch the eye of the NASCAR champion. And though, through some miracle, she had turned his head, that hadn't been enough for her. Oh, no. She had to go and set her sights on something even more evasive. His heart.

"Dammit, listen to me," he nearly shouted. "You have no idea what it's like, to live under a microscope like this. Don't come in here and try to tell me to roll over and expose my belly for these media hounds. You think they're thirsty for blood now, just let them get a whiff of something personal. You'd think they were half bulldog for the way they hang on to a sore subject."

"Sounds like you've been through it."

"Life's a bitch."

"There are hundreds of people in this garage. You act like the media is after you. Nobody else is hiding between motorcoaches or in haulers, whispering and sneaking. You bring this damn attention on yourself, and frankly, that's what is a bitch about it."

This fighting ripped at her tolerance. Her patience felt as if it had been gone over with twenty-grit sandpaper. Zander was too far gone to understand. He couldn't see it. He'd talked himself into believing the media was in some big conspiracy against him, when it was he that was feeding them, always promising that where Zander was, a story was also. She actually felt sorry for him, standing there, seeing the stony expression on his face. Stubborn ass. There was nothing she could do.

Her mind flitted back to that conversation she'd overheard at the camp, the one that had made her believe in him. "I never figured you a quitter," she said quietly. That whole speech about not giving up, about respect and determination. God, what a fallacy.

Zander's ears darkened to a deep red.

"All this time." She watched his face, knowing that if he gave himself away, it would be with a clench of a jaw muscle or tic of his eye. "I thought you were a winner. But instead of competing, you're running away. The media's just an excuse—and it's a violent circle. You disrespect their job and they get even by disrespecting your private life. You've caused it—and you can fix it. But you won't. Will you? Because it's so much easier to pretend Zander Torris doesn't have a heart and is beating up on the poor reporters for some misaligned vendetta that likely doesn't even involve them."

She lifted an eyebrow, not letting him know that she was dying inside at his lack of so much as a flinch. "Grow up."

With that, she walked the rest of the way to his motorcoach and stood there, waiting for him to unlock the door.

He did, holding the door while she climbed the steps and made her way toward the back of the coach. "You're wrong. You don't know me."

"You're right," she responded, holding on to control with every ounce of strength she had left. If she cried, if her voice even trembled he'd chalk up her entire speech to PMS or something stupid. Oh hell, what would that matter? Still, she tossed her hair over her shoulder and maintained her posture. "You won't let me."

Biting her lip, she gathered up her luggage, barely opened since she'd arrived. It was everything she could do to *not* look at the bed where they'd shared incredible sex—where Zander had let down his guard and been the man she knew he could be. Caring, warm, real.

"What are you doing?"

"I'm leaving."

"No you're not." His frame nearly filled the narrow hallway, guaranteeing that she couldn't physically pass. But the lines of his forehead made her half sob. Damn her for thinking his frown meant he didn't want her to go. She should know better. He was used to getting his way—especially with women. That was just a spoiled boy pout, nothing else.

"Listen," she said as she walked up to him. "You're not going to bully me, convince me, bribe me or otherwise seduce me into staying. I'm exhausted, and have far overstayed the welcome you never really did extend to me. It wasn't your idea I came remember, just some dumb matchmaking plan Selma got into her head."

"But—"

"Don't beg. It's not macho. The media might be watching."

His face tightened, his eyes went black. The look he gave her was cold enough to freeze any tears and send them back to where they originated. He opened his mouth as if to speak, then closed it again. She closed her eyes as he turned and stomped out of the coach, slamming the door behind him.

How *dare* she?

It would have been less fucking painful if she would have removed his testicles with toenail clippers. Worse thing was, he wasn't sure precisely what pissed him off the most. Maybe that she dared to question him. She had no *clue* what it was like every day with microphones and recorders thrust in his face. Gritting his teeth, he circled around the motorcoach.

The thunder of the cars racing side by side at two hundred miles per hour on the two and a half mile track that surrounded him mirrored the rage that pounded within him. He felt as if every time those cars made a pass, they were rolling over his gut. How had she done that? All he wanted to do was protect her, so she didn't have to face the scrutiny, the questions, the humiliation of having to see her face in the papers or trash magazines. Hell, before the month was out they'd have made up some story about her past, have them married and her pregnant with an alien kid or some other equally impossible shit. It was ridiculous. When he took her to that dinner Wednesday night, he hadn't really cared enough, and figured the cost of the dress more than made up for the inconvenience of dealing with the media for a few days until they caught the scent of another story and left her alone.

Why did he care so much now? How the hell did she get to him? Not only had she gotten to him, but she'd gotten him to open up. Had he been so easy to read? She'd tossed those accusations like well aimed missiles. She'd blown holes in his façade. Damn her. Damn it all.

But she was wrong.

He swung at the side of his coach, intentionally missing it by inches. He had a race to win tomorrow—and broken knuckles wouldn't be wise. He shouldn't even be out here. He should have walked away, went back to work and not thought another minute of it.

But he did. She was wrong. About him quitting. There wasn't a cell in his body that knew how to give up. What good would it do to spend all his energy launching a campaign against the media that wanted to taunt him? He had fun—keeping them guessing, turning last week's story into a lie and giving them another red herring to toy with while he went about his business on the track.

What else had she said? Oh, that bit about him having a heart. That was low. Of course he had a heart. He loved kids and did as much for them as possible. He took care of his crew, their families, even though it wasn't directly his responsibility. He even took care of the women he allegedly dated. While there were plenty of fine looking women who would be more than willing to see to his every whim—*every whim*—he searched out those who understood the game he played, and were willing to play along. It was easiest that way. No one got hurt. If that wasn't proof that he cared about other's feelings, he didn't know what was.

He fisted his shirt over his sternum and swallowed. And if he didn't have a heart, what the hell hurt so bad?

Thing was, it was better if she left. He could concentrate on the task at hand without worrying. Okay, so he *was* possessive dammit, but for good reason. She'd never been on this side of the track. He was just concerned she'd get taken advantage of.

Who was he kidding?

He closed his eyes, took a deep breath and leaned against the side of his motorcoach. He couldn't remember thinking so much in his life—especially over a woman. Hell, he even sounded pussywhipped, analyzing all this shit the way he was.

The bottom line was simple. There was no solution that would make everyone happy. Not that he knew what Molly wanted. Considering she had babbled on about him facing the truth and being himself, he'd bet his race earnings she'd lie if he asked her to tell him exactly what she had hoped to gain out of his weekend.

The door of the coach snapped closed, causing him to tense. *Let her go,* one side of him said. *Make her understand,* the other side argued.

He stepped around the corner to see her struggling with her bag. "Molly," he said, causing her to stop and sigh. He hated that it made him feel like she was barely tolerating him.

"What?"

"Just wait. The race isn't even halfway over yet, then we're going to go out for final practice. When that's over Selma can get you a ride wherever you're going."

"Home."

He winced. Somehow he thought she'd stay for the race. "But it's Talladega," he said. "You can't miss it."

"I won't. I have cable."

He looked her up and down, wishing like hell he had some clue how to handle this. Her temper seemed to have faded, but from the sparks in her eyes, he knew she'd ignite again with just the right amount of friction. She'd likely be a demoness in bed when in a mind state like she was right now. Shame he'd never get to find out.

"I'm sorry," he said, realizing he meant it as soon as the words left his mouth. "I…" He shoved his hands into his pockets and kicked at a loose rock on the asphalt. "I'm…just sorry."

"Me, too," she admitted. Her face softened just a little, but she still hoisted the bag higher and looked off toward the garage. Sorry wouldn't keep her here. He wasn't capable of giving her what it would take. Rich and famous as he was, he couldn't afford Molly Freibach.

"Give me that bag. Heaven forbid the media see me letting you carry your own luggage, they'll really crucify me then."

Her lip wobbled. Just enough to allow him the ability to breathe. "Don't say it," he interjected before she could respond. "I know you think I deserve it, but since you think I need to be more…truthful, then let me at least display my manners here."

The roll of her eyes made him almost feel like chuckling, especially when she passed over the heavy bag with a sigh. But that didn't change that she was leaving.

Molly watched—if one could call her meditative-like state watching—the rest of the Busch race from the crowded infield bleachers. Her mind was stir crazy, replaying and over-analyzing everything that had happened in the last day. Felt like a week. No wonder she was exhausted. Not to mention emotionally drained.

She filed off the bleachers when the race was over, chiding herself that she didn't even know who won. Talladega. So what that it was a Busch race. She'd practically been on top of the action, including a multi-car pile up coming off the corner and she'd actually only absorbed about five minutes of it.

Who was she to complain to Zander about being himself when she was acting completely out of character? Unlike him, however, she had legitimate excuses. She was tired. They'd gotten precious little "real" sleep the night before, and she'd had a long day leading up to it—both physically and emotionally draining. Today hadn't been much of a relief from that. She stifled a yawn and decided that since there were still several hours before she'd be able to leave, she could sneak back to Zander's motorcoach and grab a nap on his couch. Surely he wouldn't begrudge her that.

The garage was milling with people. She threaded her way through the rainbow of uniform colors until she got to the Team Transpro bay. She stopped short, just at the doorway and out of the way, suddenly struck by the reality of where she was. Steve and Zander stood at the front of the car near the tall toolbox, talking. Judging from the intense expressions—lined foreheads, narrowed eyebrows, terse nods, she knew it was one hundred percent shop talk. The gestures Steve made with his hands, holding them up the way two cars would race on the high banking, kept her from interrupting them.

Three crew members consulted checklists and went over the car. In the bays all around, the same rituals were being performed. Above the ruckus of voices and the clang of tools against metal, the loudspeaker squawked out the rundown of the recently completed race.

She could only go by her own experience—watching this all unfold on television, and she didn't really have time to tune in for practices and qualifying. Normally just the race, and more times than not, it was on the radio. Her senses were in overload, and only part of that could be attributed to the man standing less than fifteen feet from her.

Still, she knew it'd be several minutes before they could roar out onto the track for practice. This weekend had an unusual schedule. Selma had explained to her. There was so much going on, they'd moved final practice for the Cup cars until after the Busch race. It made for a hectic day for those drivers who did double duty.

She could hear the winner of the Busch race being interviewed over the loudspeaker. In just a few minutes she would get to experience something she never had, but always wanted to do. She could breathe in the scent of the cars, the oil and fuel, burnt rubber and hot metal. She could hear the cars rev—and boy was that different than on TV. Here, her chest vibrated with the power of so many horsepower rumbling, even in idle.

Nobody could stand here and be unaffected. This is what she had come for. She could sit across the table from her dad and play gin rummy and tell him about it all. No way was she going to let her feelings for Zander blur it all out the way she had for the Busch race. That was her own fault.

Damn shame she wouldn't be here tomorrow.

Her eyes drifted back to Zander, pulled there by a force she knew she couldn't fight. It was normal. Zander filled a room with his presence and seemed to attract women like moths to a light. Her feelings had little to do with the enjoyment she got from watching him, the way his expression changed as he spoke, the impassioned glint in his eyes that turned them nearly black with emotion. She let her gaze slip lower and admired the width of his shoulders, emphasized by the firesuit he'd somehow found time to change into.

Even when her mind shouted *stop looking* and her heart tried to remind her of the pain he was causing her, her body reacted to his physique. Remembering how the hard plain of his chest had felt against her body, how those muscles had jumped beneath her exploring fingertips made her brain tune out everything except him.

The sound of them rolling the car out of the garage stall and toward pit lane snapped her out of her reverie. Zander's car. Not a show car like the ones she'd seen of several other drivers at displays near her hometown, but an honest-to-god ready to race stock car. It sent a shiver up her spine to realize this wasn't a dream.

When the crowd closed around the car, blocking it from her view, she turned back to find Zander looking at her with an empty, longing stare.

Or at least, that's what she thought the look was. As soon as their gazes had met, he blinked and all signs of emotion erased from his features.

She forced her lips to tilt upwards, then looked away. Did it really matter if he felt something for her? Their lives were so different. He spent most of his time hiding behind the race car driver bad-boy persona. His schedule was horrendous and he had all but made it clear that he wasn't interested in doing anything that exposed his personal side, which pretty much knocked out any chance at a relationship. And what if he did propose it? Then what? She leaned against the outside of the garage and sighed. She had a job, one that she wasn't going to give up to follow some NASCAR driver around the circuit.

"Coming?" Zander's hand smoothed over her arm and grasped her elbow, all but pulling her with him.

"I can walk."

"Yeah, but you'll walk away."

"So?" she challenged. "Does it matter?" Lifting her chin, she looked him straight in the eye. Maybe she'd had a bit of a meltdown earlier, but she'd recovered, and she wanted to make sure he knew about it.

Game face in place, Zander simply lifted an eyebrow and led her toward pit row. She let him. Making a scene with all these people milling around didn't seem like a good idea and dammit, she *did* want to experience this. Soon he'd be in the car and she could breathe again.

"Zander Torris, can we have a moment?" A man stopped directly in front of them, forcing them to stop or plow into him.

"Excuse me." Zander wrapped his fingers around her arm and steered her around the reporter.

He didn't give up so easily. "You've had to give up your second place starting position because of an engine change. How do you think that'll affect your chances?"

"It won't," Zander answered, even as he increased his pace.

"Is she your good luck charm?"

Zander turned around and stopped, nearly causing her to trip and fall. "Excuse me?"

"It's Molly, right?" the photographer asked, his lips curling into a sickening smile as his eyes raked over her body. He was rather nerdy looking, but that gaze made her feel dirty.

"Forget her name."

"Does this mean you're off the market, Zander?"

"No," Molly cut in. "You can let all his female fans out there know that Zander Torris is still one hundred percent available. I did him a favor earlier in the week and accompanied him to a dinner for a charity we both sponsor and in return, he's allowed me to tag along with him this weekend. The track is fabulous, isn't it? I'm so excited to be here."

Zander looked at her, eyes wide, mouth open. She turned, using the momentum to kick him in the shin and kill the shocked look on his face. "C'mon, Zander, weren't you going to give me an overview of what happens during practice?"

The reporter turned to his cameraman, who was hastily taking pictures of the two of them. Molly didn't care. The look on Zander's face had been worth every minute of it. If he wanted to play up to the media, well, so could she. It was for exactly the same reason—to protect her already shattered heart.

Chapter Twelve

"Sit up there. With Steve." Zander waved in the general direction of the seats mounted to the pit box and turned back to what his car chief was saying. He'd raced Talladega for several years now, but the track never failed to awe him. He needed his head on straight, his mind focused to keep from making a slip up here. The track forgave little, and when racing at speeds touching two hundred miles per hour just inches from several dozen other cars, well, there was no room for error.

Whatever had possessed her to jump ahead of him and answer that reporter had knocked him totally off balance.

"I want you to draft with the other Chevys," his crewman was saying. "Try cars from the different stables to see how they're hooked up. Then switch to Fords and finally Dodges. We want to get an idea if one model gives you any better downforce, or just the opposite."

"Gotcha," Zander answered as he slipped on his heel guards. The metal shell of the car wouldn't get blistering hot today, but it certainly would tomorrow. He preferred to practice the same way he'd race— just so he'd have a good, honest feel of the car.

"Aw, shit," he said when he noticed Molly had taken his advice and climbed up beside his crew chief. She slipped on the headset like she'd done it dozens of times before. The last thing he needed was to realize she was listening to him while he was driving. It'd only be worse if she decided to talk to him while he was in there, trying to work.

"What?"

"Nothing." His crew—damn near all of them—were already giving him crap about Molly's presence. Shame they hadn't heard her basically sum up her whole reason for being here with a nonchalant comment about a favor. He hated to admit she was genius for saying it—if she'd only meant it as a front. She'd gotten to him, he'd already accepted that like a bad diagnosis from his doctor. But it still surprised him how much it hurt to hear her trivialize their time together.

With renewed determination, he climbed into the car and affixed the steering wheel. As he did several times every race weekend, he adjusted his earpieces and shoulder harness and then slipped his helmet over his head. It was hot as hell, but he long ago realized the media were less likely to interview him if he was hidden behind the smoked lens of his helmet.

"Mike check," he said, pressing the button on his steering wheel to cue the microphone.

"Gotcha, Z," his crew chief answered.

Zander shifted to get comfortable in his seat. Not that he could move much. The seat belt was actually a five point harness, and then he had the head and neck restraint that basically chained his helmet to his shoulders, preventing his head from snapping forward—and breaking his neck—in the event of a hard hit. And there wasn't any such thing as a soft hit here at 'dega.

In a few minutes, his crew would put the window net up and his visibility would be limited to what was directly out the windshield. He'd have to depend solely upon his spotter to know what was beside or behind him. He had a mirror, but it couldn't give him positions of the vehicles that raced all around him.

Letting someone else be his eyes had been one of the hardest things to accept coming to the upper ranks of NASCAR. The safety equipment was completely necessary—one could understand sacrificing visibility for something that would save a life, but the trust factor took a little more getting used to.

He blew out a lungful of air and flexed his fingers around the steering wheel. In front of him, about ten other cars sat on the grid. He watched the crews dodge around them, looking over the lines, the tires and even leaning in to talk to the drivers who, like him, had gotten in the car to mentally prepare.

This was the final chance to get this car perfect. He needed to be completely aware of everything his car did, each push, rub, and wiggle. His crew chief was counting on him to relay information back— expecting him to practically see the air as his car cut through it. He'd done it dozens of times.

Today, it might as well be his first time because he was nervous as hell.

Because of Molly? How dumb was that?

"You ready, Z? Remember, take it easy for a few laps and watch that water temp. I want to play with the tape on the nose for downforce. I'll have you come in in a few laps and we'll try taking a piece off and getting those numbers."

He blinked and eyed the water temp gauge. Anyone not familiar with the sport would never believe one six inch piece of duct tape could mean the difference between winning the race or ending up in the garage three hundred miles in with a blown engine. "I hear you," he responded.

The signal to fire engines didn't come soon enough. He rolled out with his group of vehicles and began a pace lap. In another lap or two, he'd be at full speed and hopefully could outrun thoughts of Molly. Nothing. Nothing ever had screwed his concentration the way that woman did.

It took Zander three good laps before his concentration belonged to him again. He rattled off oil and water temps to his crew, acknowledged his spotter and played the drafting game with several of his friends and competitors.

Fifteen minutes in, his crew chief called him in.

When he'd hit his marks on pit road and the crew changed his tires—it was common to scuff up a few pair of tires for race day—and they changed the position of the tape on the nose, he cued his radio. "How'd those times look?"

"Steve said you're just about a quarter second off of your qualifying time," Molly responded.

Who the hell let *her* become involved with this? Wasn't she supposed to be a spectator? "Thanks," he said dryly, straining with limited movement to see where the hell Steve was and why he didn't answer his question.

"You looked great out there. Makes me wish you could give me a ride."

Through the windshield, the crewman taking tape off his front end shot him a look. He couldn't see his smile, because of the mandatory pit road helmets, but he knew he was giving him one of those "Oh yeah, you'd like to ride her," grins.

"That wasn't part of this weekend's fan experience, Molly. Sorry." He said it as coldly as he could. Mainly because the last thing he needed was thoughts of sex with her mucking up his concentration. He couldn't help, however, throwing her "favor" comment back in her face.

"Go about twenty more laps, Torris. We're looking to see those numbers drop, but watch your temp," the scratchy voice of his crew chief came through the headset.

"Yeah," he answered. He wanted to rip those speakers right out of his ears and just take the car as fast and hard as he could around that track. In and out of traffic, without a care about temperature or tire wear or how many laps he did. He wanted to burn rubber—and burn her out of his mind. It pissed him off that he couldn't simply erase her.

When the jack fell, he crushed the pedal to the floor and left his pit box in a white plume of tire smoke.

"Take it easy, Zander. Last thing you need to do is blister up those tires," Steve barked.

"Sorry."

Molly cringed as she heard the bite to Zander's single word of apology. He was pissed. At what? Her? Why would he be? Maybe his times weren't what he wanted.

At Steve's bidding, she wrote down the lap times for each circle he made of the track. From her seat—one she'd never expected to occupy—she could only see his car when it came down the front tri-oval, and then it was little more than a colorful blur accompanied by a rush of air and a sound more powerful than thunder.

It was enough, she tried to convince herself, to be here as a fan. She really was nothing more than that. Zander hadn't expected her, and from that, couldn't she deduce he didn't want her here? It was like a broken record, repeating in her head, over and over. Typical for her, trying to overanalyze motivations and emotions. Her co-workers teased her that she missed her calling—she should have been a shrink. Now she understood what they meant.

His laps ended quickly. She stayed up on the pit box and removed the headset. He and Steve were in discussion of the car's behavior and she had no desire to join that conversation. In fact, when she'd heard they were going to park the car, her hands had gone clammy. This was it. She was going to leave. She sat there on the pit box, watching the cars still practicing zip past, listened to the roar of the crowd that had stuck around after the earlier race to see the practice. Down pit lane, air guns whirred as teams changed tires. Her senses were overloaded, yet her eyes were once again drawn to where Zander bent his head near Steve's to discuss their practice.

Molly nearly screamed when she felt a tug on her pant leg. Holding one hand over her heart, she looked down into Selma's laughing face. "You scared me!"

Selma nodded, her eyes twinkling. She pointed to her ear, then shrugged. Talking would be damn near impossible with the roar of the cars still practicing.

"I can't get you out of here tonight. I know—"

"Oh my God!" Molly watched in horror as a car careened down pit road and slammed into the back of Zander's car. The crush of metal was horrid, but the thud against the concrete wall and scream of pain from the man trapped between the car and the concrete made the hair on the back of her neck stand up.

"Shane, no!" Selma shouted.

Molly jumped over a pair of tires, nearly tripping herself on the air hose as she fought to get to him. His crew was there already, supporting his body. Molly's stomach twisted and Selma gasped as they got close enough to see the blood splatters on the white concrete.

Molly pushed a couple of crew members and one NASCAR official out of the way as she tried to get a better look at the angle of his leg. The fender was bent, and Steve was shouting to his crew to get the car off him.

"Wait," she cried out. One official tried to pull her back, telling her the paramedics were coming.

"I'm a nurse. Someone give me a rope or something. Tie it around his thigh. We have no idea how much blood he's losing." She started barking orders, despite never having taken the lead in a trauma like this in her life. She'd trained however, and there was no way she was *not* going to do her best to save his leg. "Give me a flashlight."

Someone passed her a light and she shone it down the narrow crevice between the wall and the car. Beside her, Shane continued to moan. His face was pale, his eyes glassy. He was going into shock. That might be good, because it was going to hurt like hell when they finally moved the car away and blood rushed to his leg.

"It looks bad," she said to whoever would listen. The noise of the cars on the track had stopped. The silence was unnerving. "Looks like the rim of the tire is cutting into his leg, possibly his foot or ankle too."

How were they going to get the car away from the wall without dragging along his leg? It's not like they could simply pick it straight up and move it. "We've got to get him out of there."

"Get jacks." Zander got between Josh and Shane and supported his crew man. "I'll hold him up. Get several jacks under the car and start raising it up. Slowly."

The paramedics arrived and cleared the area. Molly stepped back to let them do their job. Her heart pounded and her skin was coated with a fine sheen of sweat. She couldn't tear her eyes off the grotesque scene before her with the man pinned to the wall. What if it had been

Zander? She pressed her fist to her chest to push away the pain that balled up there.

"Molly!"

She turned to see Zander beckoning for her. The look on his face stole her breath. They were trying to move the car. The whole procedure was taking way too long. Shane had lost consciousness. The paramedics braced him against part of the backboard, ready to slide it down his length as soon as he was freed.

"Will you do something for me?" Zander asked, grabbing her hand. "Please, go with him. I can't go, Selma doesn't have the stomach for it and he doesn't have anyone here. They're going to airlift him to the hospital."

"Um." She bit her lip and looked over at Shane. Then back at Zander. His emotions were unguarded. Furrows creased his forehead but he leaned forward to touch her cheek with a gentle caress.

"Forget earlier. I know the last thing you owe me is a favor, but Shane's like a brother to me. Can you do this?"

She shivered at his touch, his words. Newsmen had surrounded the entire Transpro team. She heard them repeatedly call Zander's name, vying for his attention. For once, he ignored them and his face didn't slip into that blank mask he normally wore in front of the camera.

Molly watched as they moved the car—just enough to free Shane's trapped legs. The paramedics moved quickly, but she could see by the widening of one's eyes that he didn't like what he saw.

One of the EMT's barked the order, "Get him up on the board."

Zander released her then, but not without a quick squeeze. The pleading question was there in his eyes when she glanced back at him.

She nodded. He'd asked from his heart—he wanted her to do this for him, not for the fans or the media.

She hadn't been wrong. A man she could love—no, a man she did love—lurked beneath the surface of the NASCAR champion. She reached up and pressed her fingers to her cheek where he had touched her. He had reached out for her at that point and the media be damned if they had seen him.

Such a small victory. Too little too late. But she'd accompany Shane to the hospital, and from there, head home.

Zander watched Molly jog to catch up with the paramedics as they wheeled the stretcher toward the waiting ambulance. They'd drive to the helipad and get Shane to a hospital where he'd get the best treatment. He was confident he'd left him in capable hands.

He looked down at his palms and clenched them. He'd nearly let her slip right through his fingers. It ached as if he had. In just a couple of days, Molly had come to mean as much to him as his own crew—perhaps even more, having touched his heart in a way he hadn't since...

He shook his head. Thinking like that would just piss him off again.

Glancing up at the cameras and media holding out microphones and tape recorders, trying to get their piece of the story about this tragic pit road accident. It was their job, yes, but it seemed to dehumanize the truth here.

Good God. Shane. They hadn't told him—any of them—anything. Still, it couldn't be good. The man's leg had been pinned between his car and the wall. Nausea churned in his gut as he fathomed the pain, the horror of that feeling.

He could hear Steve behind him, his voice cracking as he explained to someone—likely one of the television reporters—that they weren't worried about finding a substitute. The entire crew was more worried about Shane's diagnosis and recovery.

That's right. Zander rubbed his hands through his hair and stood up, knowing he had to face the media. But first, he wanted to talk to his crew. "Guys," he called, motioning Steve and the rest of them to him.

When they joined him, he pulled them into a huddle. "You all know as well as I do that Shane wouldn't want us to waste time worrying about him. He's in capable hands. He's a competitor. We all are. Hell, he's probably in that ambulance right now worrying about what that wreck did to the aerodynamics of the car and wishing he could be here to get it fixed."

Zander looked around, meeting everyone's eyes before continuing. "We're already going to the back of the field to start. Our work is cut out for us now with the front and rear damage. But we can do this. We're gonna win tomorrow for Shane, right?"

"Aye!" the team shouted back at him with fists pumping the air.

Steve nodded to Zander, then clapped his hands. "Let's get her back in the garage."

Zander waited for the guys to push the car down pit road and behind the wall before turning to the media. He formulated a little speech in his head to tell them about Shane—one not unlike the pep talk he'd given his guys. He just prayed they didn't ask him about Molly.

"Hey," he called as he entered the waiting room. Everything he imagined himself saying exited his memory banks as she swung her feet off the chair and turned to him. She was rumpled, likely having fallen asleep in some uncomfortable position. She didn't bother to try to smile.

"Hi." She dropped the magazine onto the pile beside her chair. "He's in surgery."

"I know." He sat beside her, barely fighting the urge to pull her into his arms. And what? Apologize? Take her out of here? Thank her? Nothing seemed to convey the real reason he wanted to hold her. He twisted his ball cap in his hands instead. "I'm surprised you're not in there, assisting or whatever."

She laughed, though there wasn't much heart in it. "I don't do surgery."

"Ah." He swallowed and stared at his hands. He had come to see her—and get answers about Shane. But in four words he had realized how little he knew about the woman who consumed his every thought.

"I talked to Shane before they went in," she said. She kept her gaze focused on the dark TV. "He was worried about tomorrow. He kept apologizing."

"For what?" Zander couldn't believe it. "It wasn't his fault."

She waved her hand but her expression changed little. "I bet all the guys would say the same thing. They don't want to let you down."

He thought about that for a moment, and realized she was right. He didn't like it, but he couldn't deny it either. He was far more worried about Shane than tomorrow's race. And more worried about what he was going to do about Molly.

First things first. He had to know. "Will he recover? Can they fix his leg?"

"I think so," she nodded, looking at him and smiling—a smile that warmed her eyes. "He might have a limp because his ankle is pretty shattered. They're putting a rod in his shin because one of those bones broke and went through the skin."

Zander breathed. It was all he could do. At least some of the dread lifted from his shoulders. Last thing he wanted to do was carry around the guilt that one of his guys had lost a leg. "Shane's tough. He'll heal."

"Yeah, he will."

She averted her gaze again. "You wanted me out of the way, didn't you? Away from the media."

"No!" he said, probably too loudly. God, he hadn't even thought about it. He'd been worried about Shane dealing with this alone, and Molly being a nurse had made it seem the perfect solution. "I hadn't even thought about that. Screw the media. This was about my crew."

"Yeah."

Anger boiled up in him. "Then why'd you come? Because of Shane or because I had asked you to? You've no interest in either of us, according to what you said earlier. This is just some vacation weekend."

"I came because it was the right thing to do. Unlike you, Torris, I could care less what the media thinks of me. Let them say I'm your lover, your girlfriend or your latest piece of ass. I don't care if they dig into my past or try to smear my name. Because the people who care know who I am, and I don't have anything to hide and I certainly have no desire to play games with them." Fire blazed in her eyes. Her fists were clutched on her lap, the knuckles white.

"I didn't care today. Cameras rolled, microphones were shoved in my face and I didn't care. I was worried about Shane."

"Good...good." She took a deep breath, then got up and paced the otherwise empty waiting room. "I've got a question for you."

Zander put his cap on and leaned back a little. He couldn't relax with the tension between them thicker than ice in the Antarctic, but he didn't have to let her see how affected he was by it. "Ask away."

"Why?"

"Why what?" Any other time he'd focus on the sway of her hips as she walked the length of the room and back, wishing he were that denim that so snugly slid around her ass and between her thighs. While the thought flitted through his mind, he was more interested in talking to her, making things better between them than feeding an empty fantasy.

"Why are you so damn obsessed with the media? Forgive me for not knowing every nuance about Zander Torris, other than you've tattooed that bad boy title on yourself from beginning."

"I'm not any worse than any other driver. I just get caught doing it." He felt like chuckling, but knew this conversation was serious—and a lot deeper than discussing his reputation.

"You know what I'm talking about. You feed them, hell, you *told* me you do and do it intentionally. You hide—" She put up a hand, shook her head, then dropped into a chair close to him. "Never mind. This is useless."

"Why is it useless? You have questions." Questions he didn't want to answer, but he couldn't help it. His heart twisted with the knowledge that she was giving up. "What do you want to know exactly, what the media did to me? Why I torture them with half-truths and innuendos? Why I hide my private life as much as I can?"

"Yeah," she challenged back. Their voices were raised, and judging from the spark in her narrowed eyes, so were their tempers. He wanted nothing more than to shake Molly's shoulders and make her understand what the media could do to her, to them.

But that didn't matter, did it? They weren't a couple, so the media couldn't break them up. He twisted the ring on his finger. It mattered. It hurt, so it had to matter. The pain was as real and fresh as the day it was that Lana told him she couldn't take it anymore, packed up her things and moved out.

"My rookie year," his voice cracked. "I was engaged to this wonderful woman. I wanted her by my side all the time. Every race, every practice, she was there with me. She motivated me after a bad week, beat me up when I wondered if I was good enough for this sport, celebrated with me when we surpassed our goals."

He looked away. That glimpse of pity on Molly's face was almost too much to take. He didn't want that, dammit. Didn't want her to feel sorry for him! "The media started questioning our relationship. Not the TV or radio—you know they're clean shooters and don't care about personal life. Those tabloids that were just starting to exploit athletes alongside the celebrities they love to bash. Right there, next to the latest Hollywood break up, they'd run an article about me cheating, or her cheating, or her being in it for the money, or any number of other farfetched bits of stupidity."

He chuckled at Molly's wide-eyed look. No one ever believed it could be so bad.

"I'm serious. Stupid as that sounds, it happened. Every fucking week there was another article. I ignored them, but I guess she couldn't. She finally said 'enough' and left me."

"Zander, I'm so—"

"I don't want your pity. Don't be sorry. I want you to understand why I do what I do. I will never allow them to interfere in my personal business. They'll take pictures of me getting a kiss from a female fan— and you know it happens—and turn it into some secret lover plot. Hell, I think they even suggested I had kids out there. Several of them."

She blinked at him, a look of shock and horror on her face. That was better than pity, or before that, no emotion at all. "That was five years ago, Zander. Why do you continue to fight this way?"

"I won't let them hurt me again."

"If you say so."

He leapt from his chair and crossed to the window where she'd stopped. She didn't even turn.

"Get mad at me if you want. The people around you aren't pawns and your goal in life shouldn't be to trick the reporters for those magazines and papers that everyone knows make up their own stories anyway. It's just an excuse for you to hold on to the pain, because you can control it, and never let anyone else get close to you."

"You have no idea what you're saying."

She lifted an eyebrow and looked at his reflection in the glass. "Of course I don't. I've only been your arm candy, your lover, someone you owed a favor to and now a nurse who can sit with your friend at the hospital. The thing is, Zander. You don't know what you're saying—or doing. Have you considered how I feel? Did you talk to—"

"Lana."

"Lana. Did you talk to her and understand how she felt before it got to be too late?"

"Leave her out of this."

She ignored his warning. "Why? She's the whole reason you've done this. But you know what? I don't care. I don't have to live with it, you do. You have to face being alone because heaven forbid the media think you care for someone. You have to put on a face and surround yourself with props to keep them guessing. It's your life. I'm just a nurse you met at camp."

"You're more than that."

She half-laughed and turned away. "I'm going to see if they have anything to eat downstairs. If I truly was more than that, Zander, would you chase me away yourself just to keep the media from doing it?"

He stood there, staring after her as she walked out of the room. He swore there had been tears in her eyes as she whirled around, but the angle of her chin and straightness of her spine made her words hit him with more power than a two and a half ton race car bouncing off the inside retaining wall.

He let her go. He wanted to go after her, to deny it, to tell her the words she wanted to hear, but he couldn't. She was right. His reaction to everything he'd done—everything she'd done in the short time she'd been here, had been based on the tabloid reporters that seemed to be lurking at every corner. But she didn't understand. At this stage of the game, if he gave them a seed for a story, they'd turn it into a tree. There didn't seem to be a way out of this.

He sat there with his head in his hands and tried to think of a solution.

Molly walked past the hospital cafeteria and stood outside the automatic doors. Her heart was still racing from the confrontation she'd had with Zander. At this point, it didn't matter if he agreed with what she said, or if it made him pissed at her. It was the truth.

She didn't feel like eating. It had just been an excuse to get out of that small room. The hours since she'd gotten to the hospital had dragged on, and she'd had way too much time to think. To remember the look in Zander's eyes as he had asked her to go with Shane, the way he'd held her hand. It was the first time he'd completely ignored anyone watching them and just been himself. It gave her hope. For about twenty minutes.

Then she replayed the whole damn weekend in her head and found herself back at the same realization she had when she'd made up her mind to leave. When he walked in, she forgot all those reasons not to be enamored by him. Once again, his face had been free of that mask he wore for the cameras. In fact, she could have sworn she'd seen a warmth in his eyes, almost as if he cared. What it wouldn't be like to have him look at her like that always.

She lifted her head to the dark sky and let the slight breeze brush over her skin. "If wishes came true..." she whispered. The stars above her, barely visible for the bright city lights that surrounded them, didn't so much as twinkle. "Figures." Punching a few buttons on her cell, she called Selma to see about what happened next.

Chapter Thirteen

Molly never wanted to go through that again. She'd been traveling all night. There hadn't been a hotel available and Selma couldn't get the company plane to help her get home. No amount of begging was going to convince her to stay at the track one more night.

She'd left her luggage behind, trusting her new friend would see it got shipped back to her. Team Transpro had picked up the rental car tab—likely at Selma's insistence. She'd driven all the way back home, stopping only for a cup of coffee and a bathroom break. The ten hours she'd spent in the car felt like fifty. Now, sitting next to her father's old pickup, the track, Zander—everything seemed like some kind of dream. She wondered if she'd imagined half of it.

"Who's there?" her father called. He carried his cane more like a weapon than a walking aide. His face was a full frown, his eyes narrowed as he peered through his glasses at the car.

"Just me, Daddy. Missed you."

His face immediately softened, the wrinkles deepening as he smiled at her and held his arms wide. "Molly, honey, I was expecting you. What's this car?" He pointed with the edge of his cane.

"Rental. Mine's still in St. Louis. Not sure how I'll get it home." That was something to deal with tomorrow. She was too tired to think about those details right now.

"Get in here, Poppet," he called her a name he'd bestowed upon her when she was little. "Race is about to start."

Race. Ugh. "You go ahead," she told him, even though she followed him into the house. She lived in the apartment above the garage behind the house, but didn't want to be alone right now. She'd moved back to be close when her mother's health had been failing and when she died, Molly had never moved back out. "I'm not sure I want to watch."

"Like hell. You've got to. Your boy called and said to be sure to make you. Said he was gonna win one for you today."

"Whoa." Molly walked back out of the kitchen and into the doorway leading to the living room. "*Who* called you?"

"That boy you took off running after. Torris. The champ."

"Zander called here?" she repeated. Oh, this was incredible. "What did he say?"

Her father sighed. "What I just said. But that was at the end. He was too busy kissing my ass for the first half of the conversation. Figured he was asking for you to marry him or something by the way he yes sirred me half to death. Poor boy, blames himself for the way you lit out of Alabama like your tail was on fire. Something about some misunderstanding."

"Misunderstanding."

"Of course I agreed with him. Damn straight my daughter is right. That youngun' has a lot to learn. And champ or no champ, I told him so. The woman is always right. How d'ya think I stayed married to your momma for so long?"

Molly stared, unable to move. Her father, the one who never, ever asked about her dating life, social life or so much as acknowledged she should be getting married and providing him with grandchildren—the way her mother had right up until her death—was discussing her with Zander Torris as if it was a normal occurrence.

She was tired, yes, and this just made her feel like she'd stepped into a filming of Twilight Zone.

"C'mon, sit down," her father said, patting the couch beside him.

Molly looked at the TV. They were doing driver interviews. She totally wasn't interested in seeing *that* Zander right now. "I'm going to make myself a cup of tea. You want something?"

"Nope."

She shook her head and ducked back into the kitchen. Her hands were accustomed to the routine and performed the task while her mind went over what her dad had said. Each time she repeated it to herself, it seemed more and more farfetched.

"You're missing him!" her dad called.

"Good," Molly muttered as she counted down with the microwave. She didn't have the patience for the teakettle today.

"He mentioned you."

Molly sat next to her father and sipped the hot, bitter liquid. "Who?"

"Torris."

"What did the reporter ask?" Oh, she bet Zander was just thrilled to have to answer personal questions when he was trying to get his mind conditioned for the race.

"He didn't ask nothing. Your boy just said he wanted to say hello to a special girl named Molly and he hoped you were watching."

"Right." That was so not Zander. Not even close. *Special girl?* Ha. *Hoped she was watching?* Lord, she didn't even want to get into explaining it all to her father—and go through the whole bad habit Zander had of intentionally baiting the media to keep them off any hint of his "real" personal life. One that didn't exist.

He must have caught wind it helped his image to sound…capable of emotion toward a woman or something. *Special girl.* Oh yeah, his promo manager had scripted that in.

She sipped her tea and watched as the cars took the checkered flag. The roar of the cars zipping under the flag stand was nothing on TV compared to what it would be like there, yet she refused to taste regret. Her father amused her. Normally he had more favorite drivers than anyone else she knew, yet today he seemed to have eyes only for Zander.

The more laps were run, the more animated he got, nearly knocking the teacup out of her hand as he leaned forward in anticipation, then dropped back against the back of the couch, tossing his arms up and shouting at Zander that he could have made the pass.

"Remember last week, boy?" her father yelled when a yellow car came up on Zander's quarter panel. "He's a rough driver. Get away from him."

"Dad," Molly admonished. "He can't see you shaking your fist and he certainly can't hear you. Relax."

"That bastard's gonna take him out, just like he did with those two cars last week. He can't pass 'em, so he wrecks 'em."

"I'm sure he didn't mean it last week, and I think Zander will take care of his own battles if something happens."

"You can bet on that."

Molly didn't need to. He spoke the truth. She kicked her feet up, more than satisfied she'd made the right decision and was spending her Sunday with the right man. Her time with Zander had been fun, but none of it had been anything remotely close to 'real life'.

She closed her eyes, deciding she could rest just for a little bit. Her father was repeating everything the announcers said anyway, so all she had to do was listen to know what was going on. And she wasn't beyond being human. A quick camera shot to the pit lane, and seeing Steve up there on the pit box made her heartbeat leap a little. She could have been there.

No. That's not where she belonged.

"Molly! Big one. *Big one!*"

She jerked up. Her father was standing, leaning forward on his cane and studying the mess of smoke on the television screen.

"Who?" she asked, blinking to bring her sleepy eyes in to focus. Her heart needed no such prompting. It was pounding erratically just imaging Zander's car taking a hard hit into the outside wall, or another car.

"A lot. It happened mid-pack."

"Damn, Dad, how long was I asleep?" There were less than fifty laps to go, according to the commentator who said they were calling a red flag to stop the cars so they could sort this one out.

"Forever. I tried to get you up when your boy took the lead, but then he got stuck back in traffic after a slow pit stop. Shame about them losing their front tire changer like that."

"Yeah." Shane was probably cussing about being laid up in a cast right now too. "Shane will recover."

"Dadburnit."

Molly closed her eyes. Her father rarely cussed, but he didn't need to. The tone of his choice of expletives said enough.

"How bad?"

"He's out. Front suspension is jacked. Looks like he got hit from behind then that eleven car came around and took off the front end."

"Great."

He was going to be pissed. She knew they kept talking about points—and every one counted. This was something that team didn't need.

"He's getting out," her dad said, though Molly could plainly see the same thing her father did.

Zander dropped the net to signal he wasn't hurt but then sat for a moment to gather his thoughts. Son of a bitch. He wanted to win this one so he could say what he needed to say in Victory Lane.

A paramedic stuck his head in the car. "You okay, buddy?"

"I'll live. Give me a minute to catch my breath." He radioed his crew with the same message, first he'd spoken to them since getting caught up in the crazy wreck.

He removed his helmet, steering wheel and unhooked the wires and hoses that attached him to the car.

After climbing out, he pasted on a smile and turned to wave to the crowd. The paramedic grabbed his shoulder and led him to the ambulance for his mandatory check-up. He turned to look back at the car. Man, what a mess. There'd be no getting back out today.

The adrenaline rush was leaving him. His shoulder was a bit stiff where he'd braced himself against the steering wheel, or perhaps had just been slammed against that side of the driver's seat. He twisted his neck, stretching the muscles there. It was normal for those to be sore, considering he was fighting some serious g-forces all day just driving. But dammit, he'd let the guys down on that pit stop, missing the cue and getting trapped behind another car. It'd cost him better than ten positions on the scoreboard—which, when they lined up double file after that caution, slapped him back in twentieth place. Right in the middle of trouble. He sighed. Nothing was going his way this weekend. Nothing.

If there was a plus to this, he could get out of here and on his way to find Molly a little earlier. But dammit, he'd wanted to prove something to her first.

"Zander, what happened out there?"

"How does this affect the points race?"

"Will you get your car back out?"

TV, radio, and print reporters deluged him as soon as he finished with his check-up and walked out of the infield care center.

"It looks pretty bad," he answered, scanning the crowd over the cameramen before turning back to the reporters. They practically fed him the microphones as they encouraged him to continue. "We had a great car and anticipated another strong finish here. But those restrictor plates—they keep us all bunched up together and when one person makes a mistake, we all pay for it. I was just in the wrong place at the wrong time. It'll hurt us a bit in the points, but we can overcome next week."

"What happened in the pits to put you back in the pack?" someone asked.

"My fault. Miscue. Shane, buddy, I know you're watching. We miss you!"

A reporter Zander knew like to stir up crap between drivers jammed a recorder toward his face. "What happened out there? Who caused it?"

"Call the network and get it on tape. Then you tell me. I saw the tire smoke, then felt the impact. Doesn't matter who did what now, it's over and we're not going to win this race."

Zander shook his head, knowing his temper was brewing just under the surface. His head was throbbing now and his shoulder needed a good rub down and an ice pack. He was just about to walk away and decline further questions when he heard a voice a row or two back ask something interesting.

"What was that? You, there in the red."

The thin, balding guy, rather soft spoken for a reporter, repeated his question. "If you could do anything differently today, or this weekend, what would it have been?"

Zander's first reaction—and probably the one he would have blurted without thought a year ago, was to ask this guy if he was suggesting he'd done something wrong.

But in the back of his head, he heard Molly's lecture about how he treated the media, and played up to them, and he realized this was exactly the question he was looking for to make a change. He knew what each of those men and women expected. They had their microphones or recorders poised, their curious eyes watching him intently.

"Do differently? You mean other than the obvious and avoid that wreck you mean?"

A guy beside him snickered. Probably because Zander had read him the riot act a time or two.

Zander didn't wait for a comment. "I would probably have given up my hobby of coming up with crap for you to write about me. Not all of you mind you, because some of you actually are willing to respect that I have a private life outside of the track. I've come to realize that I've been so busy giving you guys things to report on so you didn't know the truth about my private life that I've managed to not have time *for* a private life. Sorry, you—the media—aren't that important. It took a real special lady to open my eyes to what I was doing—and it's going to stop now."

"Zander, what about—"

"No more questions. I need to figure out how to convince someone what we had is for real."

———

Molly's heart dropped clean out of her chest when Zander looked straight into the camera and winked.

Her dad cackled with laughter. "I told you!" His body shook as if it were some hilarious joke.

Wait. Joke. Emptiness filled the spot her heart once filled. Molly breathed. "Oh, Dad." She rubbed her eyes. "Don't get your hopes up. It's all just another Zander Torris media stunt."

The phone rang.

"Don't answer it!" Molly warned.

"It might be him!"

She didn't care. "It might be a reporter. They know who I am. They can easily figure out who he was talking about."

Of course her father didn't listen to her. "Hello? Yes, yes she's right here."

Molly groaned but took the phone. Her dad was going to pay for this. "Hello?"

"Molly, it's Selma. Don't talk, I can't hear a damn thing because of the race. Listen, Z's on his way. He's lost it over you. I know you saw the TV, but you missed everything else. He did everything but give the media guys here a wedding date. He is coming to see you. I wanted to warn you. Good luck."

"Why?"

"What?" Selma screeched. "Did you say something?"

"Why is he doing this to me?"

"I can't hear you. Just be ready. He's on his way."

The phone clicked. Selma was gone. No answers, only more questions. What did it mean? Why was Zander coming? Why *did* he say what he did? Even if he had feelings, which she was doubting, what purpose did coming to Ohio prove? What message was he giving the media?

Selma had to be warning her not to let her heart get too involved in it—and to protect her from what was going to be published. Zander was using her, another ploy to keep the media on their toes.

She gritted her teeth and clenched her fists. "Dad, forget you heard any of this. Anything."

Zander was coming, and she was going to make him pay for putting her in the middle of this.

❦ ❦ ❦

Zander's borrowed Lear Jet felt slower than his car at the forty-five mph pit road speed, especially after coming down from one eighty. Couldn't they push it any faster? Was Ohio farther away than he imagined? Had the pilot gotten the wrong directions?

When they landed, he had an hour drive to look forward to. She'd better be there. Not that it would matter, he'd made up his mind and if he was one thing, it was determined. At this point he was willing to do whatever it took to convince her he was tired of the games and wanted to change his ways. For her. For them.

Not that he thought it'd be so easy. But he came prepared. Her clothes, including those he'd left in the back of his rented truck just five days before. Five days.

How the hell had his life spiraled out of control in five short days?

"Half hour, Torris," the pilot called.

"Thanks, Max," he replied, then pushed his hands through his hair. He'd finished his interviews, rushed to his coach and showered, then pulled every favor he could to get a flight north. Immediately.

He'd hope to win the race so he could proclaim his love for her— Oh Christ, just listen to his mind, he sounded like a fucking dork thinking like that, but really, what else would he call it? He was willing to stick his neck out, prepare himself for total humiliation because it was better than never seeing Molly again.

One night without her had been too much. He'd tossed and turned all night, wondering where she was, who she was with, if she was driving, if she was okay. What if something had happened? It was much more than he was willing to deal with again. He hadn't intended for it to happen, but Molly had gotten through to his heart and he'd be damned if she was going to walk out of it and leave him hurting.

So here he was, on a jet with her luggage, but nothing of his—he had no time to pack. He hadn't planned any further. It's not like he could just demand she leave everything behind and come with him, could he? She'd laugh in his face.

Shit. She had her career, her family, her own place. Selma had mentioned the same thing when he was running around, trying to get a ride.

"Are you selfish enough to expect she give up her entire life to travel with you, deal with this chaos?" she had asked.

"I'd do it for her," he insisted.

"Really?" she'd countered. He'd wanted to wipe that grin right off her face. "If she said she wanted you to stay in Ohio and be the stay-at-home-husband and father, you'd just walk away from racing and never turn back?"

"Hell no," he said.

"Well, then."

Zander growled out his frustration at her parting words and paced the length of the plane. "Dammit!"

"Everything okay back there?"

"Yeah," he answered the pilot, whose voice held a bit of humor. Humor my ass, he thought. Was there a solution to this? Was there a way for them to be together?

"Max, got an ear?"

"Sure, Zander, what's the problem? You look ready to explode."

Zander knelt behind the pilot's chair. "As you know, I'm going to see Molly. She's incredible. I don't need to get into all of that. You're married, aren't you?"

"Yep. You thinking this Molly's a keeper?"

Zander sighed. Keeper? That didn't even touch it. "I think so. Problem is, she's a nurse, more than that, one of those nurse practitioners or something. Independent woman. She volunteers at the children's camp for her vacations. How the hell do I suggest she just leave that and come with me?"

"You can't."

"Well, I highly doubt I'll be able to keep up a schedule that involves flying to and from Ohio three or four times a week."

The pilot chuckled and adjusted a few instruments. "Find her a job with the series. See if the children's ministry needs a nurse. Maybe one of the teams. Do you have a team physician?"

Zander sat back on his heels. *Hire her?* Why hadn't he thought of that? "You're a genius, Max. I need to make some calls."

"Good luck, Torris."

"Thanks." He got up, patted the pilot on the shoulder and returned to his seat. He hit Selma's number on his cell. She answered on the first ring. He'd owe her everything, and it'd be worth it if she could make this happen.

Chapter Fourteen

Molly left her dad's house before the race was even over, too upset by Zander's latest publicity stunt to care who won.

Why? It didn't make sense. She straightened up her tiny apartment and replayed everything she could think of. Nothing equaled a valid answer to "why?"

Zander had mentioned a woman. Molly had even gone online and searched archives of his past. All she found was one photo from Zander's rookie season. He'd stood beside his car, with a grin on his face bigger than any she's ever seen. He had his arm thrown around a pretty blonde girl. Not a tall, gorgeous model, but a down-home, attractive, average girl. Her name wasn't listed. But the more Molly stared at the picture, the more she understood.

The Zander in that photograph was the man she'd seen in the moments they'd had together. The light in his eye, the grin—the way it pulled slightly more at one corner of his mouth than the other.

"What a lucky woman," she muttered. Then she realized what she'd said and wished she could suck her words back in. Somehow, while trying to protect her from the press, shield her from the limelight, Zander had lost her.

It made her chest tighten to know he fought so hard because of the pain he must have gone through—the blame, the anger, the frustration.

And what of me? Her heart dared to ask. Molly paced until she was sure the carpet would wear through. At one point Zander had tried to protect her, making her think maybe he did care. But his initial intent had been to use her—hadn't he bought her clothes so she looked presentable on his arm? She was dizzy trying to make sense of his actions and see the rationale behind them.

Misunderstanding. That's the word Selma had used when she'd called. What if? Oh, God, just teasing herself with the idea caused tears to spring to her eyes. Yet hadn't she done it to herself all along, looked for hints and fantasized that he returned her feelings? Hadn't her reaction to him changed several different times over the last five days? Hadn't her own eyes been opened as she saw the various sides of Zander Torris? Did she really want to believe he could change, considering she'd all but challenged him to do just that?

Well, misunderstanding or not, it didn't change that she was back to real life and no amount of fantasy was going to fill her fridge or wash her clothes and get her ready for her shift at the hospital tomorrow morning. She'd deal with Zander when he arrived. Then move on.

Despite her determination not to overreact, her skin went clammy when she saw the strange car parked in her spot next to her dad's pickup. Damn, that was fast, Selma hadn't been kidding. If it was Zander. Could be a reporter already.

She didn't want to deal with that. She wanted to unload her groceries, do her laundry and curl up with a book until she could go to bed and throw herself back into her routine.

She snickered, though, as she imagined Zander squeezing into that purplish-color subcompact car. The fact that the car was empty was bad news. Which meant the enemy was already inside, consorting with her father.

Enemy. She rolled her eyes at herself. It wasn't quite right, but maybe for her own self-preservation she should think of him with that term.

"Whatever," she muttered. She'd let them talk. Her father was probably loving the fact a NASCAR champ was sitting across from him at the dining room table. In the meantime, she'd get her car unloaded.

On her third trip to the car from the apartment over the garage she saw the men on the back porch.

"Hi guys," she called, but only after swallowing a few times. Zander looked so...real and...normal and...non enemy-like standing there next to her father.

"Let me help with those." He cleared the three steps with one leap and pulled the case of bottled water out of her hands.

"Gee, thanks, Casanova, where were you when I had to load the car?"

"If I'd have known," he said, winking.

"Please," she answered, rolling her eyes. She couldn't imagine Zander trotting along with her in the supermarket. He'd be flirting with the other shoppers, juggling limes for the photographers and then signing autographs at the checkout, leaving her to do exactly what she did herself anyway—load her cart, then her car, then her apartment.

"This is neat, the way you stay with your dad, but don't." Zander followed her up the steps as if it was perfectly normal he'd come to visit for the afternoon.

"It works for us."

"I don't know. Your dad hinted he might like to have some buddies over for poker night or something and doesn't feel right with you watching over him."

"Oh right. He's never said anything, besides, he goes to the Legion Post couple of nights a week to play cards." Why was Zander getting in her personal business like this? Barely suppressing a growl of impatience, she took the case of water from him and placed it on the counter. "I'm never home anyway, so I doubt it matters."

"He does think you need to get your own place."

"I have my own place and you're in it. And since we're on that subject, how about you tell *why* you're in my place."

"I needed to see you. Talk to you."

"I'm listening." Maybe she shouldn't be so defensive but she was tired from driving all night. Her nerves were shot because, whether she had wanted to or not, she'd tried to figure this mess out in her head. Now he was here and she was having a miserable time not noticing how he filled the room with his presence, how his eyes roved over her like caresses, how his lips pushed up in a slight masculine pout at the sight of her crossed arms and straight back stance. It took everything she had not to let her heart lead this conversation. Because then she'd start remembering how good his mouth felt against hers when he kissed her or how his tongue tracing down the column of her throat had made her entire body shudder. And those hands… "I'm listening," she affirmed, mentally closing off *everything*.

"You were right," he started. Molly stood still while Zander paced, rubbing his hands down the front of his jeans, then jamming his fingers into his pockets. He stared at the floor, the counter, the window, anywhere but her. "I got caught up making up Zander Torris to the point that I forgot who I really was. Everything that wasn't about racing or my team was about how I'd look to the media or what story they'd write next."

She nodded. She dare not move and betray her stand. Her heart beat erratically. She was surprised he couldn't hear it. He'd listened? He was admitting she was right?

"I'm ready to change all that." Zander raised his green-gold eyes to hers.

He held his breath as he studied her face, her reaction. Her eyes widened, then darkened. Her lips parted, her gasp barely audible. She swallowed before she blinked. When she did, her emotions were erased from her features.

"I'm glad for you, Z. Very glad." She spoke slowly. Was she choosing her words to veil a question? God, he hated this. He hadn't put his heart on the line like this since…since he didn't want to remember when. It hurt to remember. Yet with Molly standing there, looking like she felt fucking *sorry* for him, well, that hurt too. Maybe this had all been a mistake.

Now that he'd made the decision to tell her, he wouldn't back down. He'd just have to believe his gut feeling. It wasn't as if he'd been very honest with her about his feelings before now. "Your dad said you watched the race with him."

"Right up until your wreck. Sorry. I know you wanted this race."

"It didn't mean anything to win without you there to celebrate with me."

"Nice try."

"Dammit Molly, you're making me nuts here. You told the media we were nothing in one breath and argued with me about being honest with them and just living my life without caring what they say in the next. Then you up and leave me, making me spend a miserable night trying to figure out just how I'm going to convince you to come back when I've got nothing to offer you but a schedule that keeps me on the road more than three quarters of the year, and a shadow of reporters that want to know what I ate for freaking breakfast. Can't you give a man a break? Women have been arm candy for the last few years. I don't let them in *my* bed, *my* house or my heart."

She looked away.

He wanted to die inside. It was like Lana all over again. Maybe worse. He stepped closer to her, trapping her between his body and the counter. Placing one hand on either side of her face, he turned her eyes up to meet his.

The raw emotion there hit his gut like a car with its throttle stuck wide open. He couldn't speak, didn't dare question what he saw. He lowered his mouth to hers and nearly wept from the pleasure of tasting her once again.

He ended the kiss and gave them both a minute to breathe. "Tell me," he whispered, "that you want me to leave and never bother you again."

One chance. He had to give it to her.

"Zander."

"Tell me," he repeated. "I'll go. If you don't tell me to go then I'll be here every week, sometimes twice a week. I didn't win a championship because I won one race—it was perseverance and I intend to pursue you with every bit as much drive."

"It doesn't matter how I feel. Even if I want you. It won't work."

"And here I thought the women were the romantic ones with their 'love will find a way' poetry and crap."

"Nothing poetic about two people who live hundreds of miles apart and who have jobs that keep them busy week in and week out. Wanting it to work and making it work are two separate things. I'm pretty realistic, remember? Sorry."

"So come with me," he said, once again watching her face as he played the trump card. He'd held his breath at the way she indirectly admitted she cared about him. Winning a race was never so rewarding.

"I can't believe you're asking that. No, never mind. You would. You'd expect me to leave this, my dad, my job, my career and what? Hide in your motorcoach for ten months out of the year?"

"Bring your dad, we'll find him a place outside Charlotte, or just let him live in the house I rarely get to see. As for your job, I've got some options for you there too. Personally I'd love to see you take on the position of staff nurse for Team Transpro racing. That way I can get that physical you denied me when I met you last week."

"Okay, so you not only want me to come hide out in your motorcoach ten months out of the year, but I'm supposed to earn my keep giving your guys physicals—"

"Only I get physicals. They get check-ups or assessments. The kind of stuff that requires they keep their clothes on."

"I see."

"And you can bring your dad."

"Uh huh. What if I said no?" Her voice was stern, but wavered with hints of laughter.

"Then I'll fly up here every chance I get, bug you at work. Oh, and I'll call every local radio and television station and make them proclaim my love at least several times a day. I'll fill the tabloids with stories of how I'm wasting away and my entire career will be in jeopardy because you won't be with me—"

"Zander!"

He shrugged. "I know you don't believe I could have changed overnight, but maybe I just needed you to show me what I was missing."

Tracing his fingers down her arm, he picked up her hand and squeezed it. "I've known you a week. I won't propose or anything crazy to really send you running, screaming, but can I at least get you to take a look at the jobs? I didn't even tell you about the proposal NASCAR is considering from the camp to work out co-sponsorship to bring a handful of kids to the tracks every week. They'll need a health care provider at all times. You know money won't be an issue, your dad will be taken care of, and we can work on showing the media what happily every after means."

"What does it mean?" she asked, smiling her answer as she tilted her head up to his for a kiss to seal the deal.

"Oh, something about riding off into the sunset or something. But I've never been good on a horse. I can rein in about seven hundred of them when they're under my hood, though. Mind if I drive?"

"I could be persuaded to consider it." She said after a long kiss that made her body tingle all over. "I can't believe you came all this way. And I'm sorry you didn't win today."

"Oh, but I did," he said, dropping a kiss to her nose and leaning his forehead against hers in a way that touched her heart more than his words did. "I got my trophy right here. My trophy girl."

Melani Blazer

To learn more about Melani Blazer, please visit www.melaniblazer.com. Send an email to Melani at melani@melaniblazer.comor join her Yahoo! group to join in the fun with other readers as well as Melani! http://groups.yahoo.com/group/melaniblazersmusings

Believe the Magic
© *2006 Melani Blazer*

When the strange antique dealer bestows Ella Mansfield with a weird necklace, proclaiming it magic, Ella refuses to believe. Why would she have a use for such a thing?

But she finds herself the target of some pretty odd characters, including the sexy but enigmatic Quentin, who becomes her guardian, her guide and her lover. Gradually she learns her necklace holds two of the ten original gems stolen from the fairy king - gems that control all the magic in the world. Ella realizes the need to believe, but even more her need to search deep within her heart to figure out who to trust, especially when those closest to her seemed to be following their own agendas.

With bad guys just a step behind them, Ella and Quentin use the magic to jump through time and space while bluffing their way out of questionable situations - in search of a plan. That comes to a screeching halt when Ella finds herself face to face with the man she's been trying to avoid.

Ella's an unlikely hero, learning as she goes - but the ultimate lesson involves a sacrifice she never expected to face, and one that all the magic in the world cannot undo.

Available now in ebook and print from Samhain Publishing.

Enjoy the following excerpt…

Feeling generous, I held the door for a man in a Chicago Bears sweatshirt.

"Thanks. Ah, wait," he said.

I paused, leaning forward to see what this guy wanted. Okay, really eager to see what this guy wanted. I hadn't seen one this live in a coon's age. "Yeeesss?"

"You're Ella, Ella Mansfield, right?" And he was asking for me. My toes tingled.

"Yeeesss," I answered again, blinking. "You are?" Only the most handsome man in the universe alive today and I want to jump your bones, cook your dinners and have your babies.

Okay, I'd admit to thinking the first thought, but added the last two just to make it not-so-cheap. My God, he looked good. In a bad boy kind of way. Hair that looked like it intentionally fell into his eyes—and those eyes. Vivid green framed by dark lashes, enhanced by thick eyebrows. Strong jaw lined with stubble. He looked the type to wear black leather or even ripped up denim. Thank God he didn't, because I don't think I'd be able to breathe faced with that vision.

"Who are you?" I repeated, desperate to get my bearing and stop ogling the customer.

"Quentin Paige." He hooked a thumb in the general direction of the corner. "Sam down the street said to talk to you."

"Oh, no, sorry. Don't want anything else Sam has to share with me."

"So you can't sell me a trip to Denver?"

I'd put my hand out, nearly touching his chest to push him back away from me, but at the word "sell" I reached a little farther and bunched my fist in the material above the Bear's logo. No sense ruining a sale. In fact, after scaring me this morning Sam owed me. "Right in here, what was your name again?" I released his shirt once I was sure he'd follow me back to my desk.

"Quentin. I know. Different. My parents were hippies, what can I say."

I nodded. "Mine were rednecks. Still are. Have a seat."

He was silent after that. I totally ignored Sara and Althea despite the holes they were drilling in the back of my head with their eyes.

They were the Saturday regulars who usually managed to make the bulk of their paycheck from those who wandered in on Saturdays. Most of their clients were the working people needing a quick escape. We were good at those.

Marnie, the boss, had taken a mini-vacation herself just this weekend. I'd get tattled on for snatching customers when she got back. Yeah, so I wasn't scheduled to work, but it's not like I just stole the customer. He asked for me. Worst that would happen was I'd have to surrender any commission I made on this one. Or ship the boss back off to Vegas for another weekend. And this time, I just might accompany her. And if I was lucky, never return. No one would miss me, at least for awhile.

"Will you be traveling alone?" I asked in my sweetest professional voice.

He glanced around and nodded. Was this a secret?

"Travel dates?"

"Now."

"What?"

"As soon as I can get on a plane and fly."

I leaned over, a mistake because I caught a load of the heavenly lure he wore as cologne. "Did you try the airport? It's a little faster to get a ticket that way on this short notice."

"They want ID. I don't have any." I studied him. He had to be at least my age, but he dressed more like a footloose college student. Must be it, I figured. Emergency run home.

"And you think I can get you a ticket without ID?"

"I know you'll help me get where I need to go."

I stood up. I needed my job. Wanted Mr. Tall, Dark and Handsome who was sitting in front of me, but he wasn't gonna cover my rent when it came due in two weeks. "Sorry. No ID, no ticket."

Quentin grabbed my hand and hauled himself to his feet. The toes of his shiny new Nikes touched the tip of my boring black ankle boots. Must be a lot of static in the air. I felt the tingles of it up and down the front of my body.

He grabbed both my hands and flipped those deadly emerald eyes in my direction. "Holy—" I said before his mouth landed on mine. I love roller coasters, but saying that's what his kiss felt like would be an understatement. Maybe I could liken it to being the roller coaster, not just riding it. When I drew back, his eyes had turned dark.

I caught my breath and tried to step back. He had my hands tightly in his. "Hey, you're hurting me." What in the heck were Sara and Althea doing anyway, charging admission? "Help me here."

"Looks like you're doing fine all by yourself," Sara jeered.

"You're doing just fine," Quentin repeated, his breath fanning against my cheek in a way that cooled my skin and set my blood on fire. That was not good. Men weren't any more abundant in my life than money, so of course I'd react this way. I drew in a breath. "I'm still not going to sell you a ticket."

"I don't want a ticket. I need you to help me in another way."

"I—"

"Shhh," he crooned. I felt like the rats in the Pied Piper, mesmerized by the spell of his once again green eyes. He lifted our joined hands to my chest. Whoa, danger zone. His eyes met mine. His stare was so intense, I couldn't look away. I tried, trust me.

The high neck of my sweater had hidden the necklace. Until now. He pulled the collar down just a bit until he could see it, and sighed, almost a lusty sound. His eyes were black again. I wanted to rip my gaze from his and check his mouth to see if he had fangs. I expected his next move to be Dracula style, leaving me drained of blood on the floor of the office. Talk about a gruesome death. Sara and Althea would really charge admission to see that.

His head didn't move closer, but his hands reached higher. He touched the bared skin just above my pulse and electricity coursed through me. From the necklace? I wanted those beads to freakin' electrocute him for scaring me this way. I held my breath.

He was smarter than that. He made me touch them, his fingers closed over mine. "Move them together."

"What?"

"Push them together. They'll slide."

He jerked my fingers toward the center. I half-expected the rope to break on the back of my neck. Or sever my head.

"Break it up, you two. There's a customer here," Althea ordered.

The spell was broken. I stepped back, shaking and feeling like I'd run a marathon. Backwards. While wearing scuba gear.

"Quentin."

The voice snagged my attention. Sam was here.

I tugged my collar back over the necklace and slid into my chair. Let Sam handle this.

"Can I help you, sir?" Althea, in her long, tight skirt, walked toward Sam, her behind twitching. I groaned and rolled my gaze back toward her intended victim. At least he was ignoring her.

"He's come after this one." I pointed at Quentin, trying to let Althea know Sam wasn't a potential customer.

"You stay out of this Ella-Mae. This one's mine."

I raised an eyebrow, but realized she was nothing. The action was happening right in front of me.

"What are you doing in here? I told you to stay away from her." Sam walked right past my co-worker and launched into Quentin.

"I need to get out of this town, man. You need to give me my stuff back."

Sam's finger tapped the still smiling Bears' logo. "What are you going to do, call the police? You've been identity diving all over the place. You realize you're causing more havoc than you've helped to avert. I may have to replace you."

"You wouldn't do that. I've got the power now."

"Not without the gems." Sam looked my way.

Quentin dove at me, landing right on me, on my chair. The chair wasn't prepared either and tipped right over.

"Blasted!" I yelped and pushed upward. Quentin popped three feet in the air above me and hung there like a side of beef in a meat locker

I laughed at the expletive that emitted from his nicely shaped mouth.

And once I realized I could think and keep him afloat, I checked out the rest of him too. I'm one to like longer hair, but his was just plain messy. I was totally convinced those weren't his clothes. The baggy sweatshirt belonged on someone about a dozen years his junior or thirty years his senior. I wondered if I could undress him while he hung there. I leaned back, still positioned in my tipped chair, and waggled my pinky. His sweatshirt rose to show off a nicely defined set of abs. "Nice," I murmured.